Text copyright © 2016 by Ella York

All Rights Reserved. No part of this book may be reproduced or transmitted in any form or by any means, electronic or mechanical, including photocopying, recording, or by any information storage and retrieval system, without written permission from the author. For information please email Rashida@Ella-York.com

York Publishing

Charlotte, NC

Visit our website at

www.Ella-York.com

First e-book Edition: November 2016

First Text Edition: November 2016

ISBN-13: 978-0692790922
ISBN-10: 0692790926

When Love Isn't Enough

Table of Contents

Dedication

Prologue

- 1) The Meeting
- 2) The Fallen Rose
- 3) The Collar
- 4) Pain
- 5) Friend Zone
- 6) Money and Happiness
- 7) A Tale As Old As Time
- 8) Feel the Energy
- 9) The Confession
- 10) You Just Show Up At My Door
- 11) I'm Tired
- 12) The Mask
- 13) El Yunque
- 14) Lust and First Sight
- 15) The Morning After
- 16) Anxious
- 17) Love at Second Sight

18) Paradise
19) This Is What It Feels Like
20) Making up is Never Easy
21) Sydney's Wine Bar
22) What's Words Between Friends
23) What's Done in the Dark

Epilogue

About The Author

Contact the Author

Coming Soon

Dedication

To my two Angel Babies (my husband and I affectionately named them Peanut, and Pepper) and my Rainbow baby Maddy, words cannot begin to express the joy that you have brought to my life. You all have changed mommy for the better and challenged me to be a better person and live without fear.

Thank you my little loves

When Love Isn't Enough

Prologue

Arya Rose

Roses... They symbolize so much - they symbolize Love. Friendship. Happiness; but what most people don't realize is that they also symbolize Pain. Sadness. Death. You see, this darkness is symbolized by the thorns that are birthed from these beautiful creations of nature.

As I sit here and reflect on life and death; I see a black rose and it's so incredibly rare. Black, the color of emptiness and darkness – the color of no light; attached to this rose. This beautiful thing that represents: love, friendship and happiness. How does that even work? Why does nature create such irony? In the midst of the darkness, there is light. In the midst of pain, there is pleasure. In the midst of death there is life.

When Love Isn't Enough

This is the story of the black rose...

My name is Arya Rose and the journey that you are about to partake in is the story of a very unique group of friends. Why are they unique? Most people are lumped into their group of friends by default because they share a common ground, or unique ancestry. My friends are unique because although we are all very different we are united by one thing... Love. That love is formed from a mutual respect that we share for one another. We could not be more different in our personal lives and views; and that is what makes us so special.

Join me as I let you into the lives of five women. Join me as I take you beneath the surface of their well-placed veils. Join me as I uncover the black rose.

Friend

Def - A person that has a strong liking for and trust in another person. A person who is not an enemy. A person who helps or supports someone.

Chapter 1
The Meeting

Arya

The day of the lunch has arrived and everyone was abuzz with excitement. The sun shone high in the sky and there was the slightest breeze in the air that lets you know fall is just around the corner. Fluffy white clouds dance across the sky; I inhale, taking in the crisp air and I am reminded about why I love the fall and why I miss it so much.

I wait inside the restaurant for my friends. Desi pulls up to the valet stand driving a bright red Maserati Granturismo. Desi's story is one of absolute rags to riches. Her parents were born and raised in Coahuila, Mexico and they immigrated here when her mother was a few months pregnant with her. With very little money and even fewer possessions, Desi was born in the United States, therefore, making her a US citizen. She went to college at the University of Minnesota and received her Bachelor's degree in Marketing with a minor in business. When I first saw Desi I remember thinking that she was stunning and wanting to meet her.

Desi was 5'5 with black wavy hair that crept down the middle of her back. She had dark grey eyes and the most dazzling smile. She stood there with a perfect physique looking at her phone; giving every woman that walked by disapproving glares as she assessed their appearance; typical Desi. I try to get her attention but she must not have seen me. She walks over to the hostess stand and mutters something that I cannot hear, sending the hostess away rolling her eyes. Desi is not always the nicest person but she is very loyal and knows how to make things happen. Desi proceeds to sit in the waiting area; watching her sit there my mind races back to the day I met her.

When Love Isn't Enough

It was my freshman year – second semester and we were sitting in our Introduction to Marketing class and the teacher was assigning us to our groups. I remember thinking I really wanted to be in a group with Ethan and Darnell; not only were they the smartest guys in our year, but they were so damn cute. Ethan had been very nice to me since the first day of class, but I always got the feeling he was trying to hook me up with Darnell. Darnell was captain of the debate and football teams, and he was also incredibly handsome. We never really said much, just exchanged flirtatious glances.

I listened to the group assignments and heard my name, *Arya, Darnell and Desi*. One out of two ain't bad, I thought to myself nodding. I didn't know much about Desi besides she was the most beautiful girl in our year. She seemed to know what she was talking about when she raised her hand in class. We sat with our groups following the announcement and received our instructions.

When Love Isn't Enough

Desi started with a proclamation "I do not care what stuff you have going on in your other classes, but this had better be a priority for you." She glared at us and not very politely continued, "this class is in my major so I need to receive an A. Being that this project constitutes for 70% of our grade you two bozos have just gained a new best friend. I am going to be all in your business for the next ten weeks."

Darnell and I sat there with wide eyes and shocked expressions; that was the first time Desi cracked a smile. We relaxed just a little bit and after a pregnant pause Desi said "But I'm serious" and all three of us fell out laughing. I knew from that moment on she would be a great friend; I love her authenticity and sassiness. Desi, Darnell and I became very close because we were always together working on that damn project.

I smile quietly to myself and chuckle thinking back on that memory. I admire Desi's knee length black dress and red Chanel bag; Desi has accomplished everything she set out to accomplish in life. I looked up as Tahj pulls up in an equally impressive car; she had recently bought a BMW – X4 sport crossover. She steps out and the sun beams off her black pixie cut. Tahj is one of the most gorgeous women that I have ever known.

She has dark skin, dark eyes, and a body for days. Her skin is the most beautiful shade of brown and she stands 5'7 without heels and 5'9 with. She is the type of girl that every man wanted. She speaks with the tiniest hint of an accent, because she grew up with her parents that were born and raised in Guinea Bissau, Africa. She is beautiful and brilliant.

I think back to the first time that I met Tahj. We were in the auditorium before our first day of classes, attending the new student orientation. She was sitting there with an equally attractive girl named Victoria. Victoria was a less impressive 5'5 stature but she knew how to command the attention of a room. She had a wonderfully caramelized skin tone and hazel eyes; with shoulder length, curly black hair that bounced as she talked animatedly. Victoria was a show stopper.

As the lights dimmed around us the Chancellor began to speak. I remember not being able to focus on what he was saying because Tahj and Victoria were making jokes. While I should have been completely annoyed, I found myself amused. When Tahj and Victoria looked up and saw me staring at them; I looked down blushing, completely embarrassed.

After the presentation was over Victoria walked over to me with a smirk on her face. Tahj just watched inquisitively. I thought she was going to let me have it for eavesdropping on them, so I started thinking of my rebuttal in my head. *I honestly didn't mean to listen in... It's just that you were so damn loud!* ... No! That would probably just get me hurt! ... *I didn't mean to. It's just your jokes were really funny and you guys are really beautiful...* No! She will just think I am weird... I let out an exasperated sigh. *Arya pull it together*! My palms started to sweat and my breathing began to hasten. I was on the verge of a panic attack when I felt someone tap me on the shoulder.

    I forced myself to look up even though my eyelids felt like they weighed fifty lbs. She really was just as pretty up-close. My mouth was dry and she just stared at me for a little while. I couldn't think of anything to say; that proved unnecessary as she reached out her hand and introduced herself. I took her hand in disbelief and shook it for a little too long. She proceeded, "My name is Victoria and that is my friend Tahj (she said pointing in Tahj's direction), we couldn't help but notice you were sitting all alone and we honestly hate to see people looking lonely and desperate. We wanted to know if you would join us for lunch?" I stood there looking like a deer in headlights; my jaw dropped. She must have been amused with my response because she suddenly dropped my hand and chuckled.

When Love Isn't Enough

This must be some sort of sick joke. Why would she want to be friends with me?

I looked up at Tahj's face for confirmation that I was dreaming; however, she looked just as confused as I was. This must not be Victoria's normal way of handling situations. I sat in silence for what felt like an eternity before Victoria rolled her eyes, grabbed my arm and told me to come with her. While we walked the ten feet over to Tahj, I stopped hyperventilating and began to regain feeling in my feet (which originally felt like they were weighted down by lead). "Tahj I would like you to meet..." Victoria paused and looked at me seemingly perplexed; "Um... what's your name? You never told me". "Arya... Arya Rose" was all I could muster up the courage to say. Tahj still looking confused extended her hand to shake mine and introduced herself.

Months later, after I had become friends with them, I asked Tahj and Victoria what Tahj's look was about when we first met. She laughed and told me that Victoria kept saying agitatedly, "What is her problem?" during the presentation. She thought that Victoria was coming over to tell me off. So when Victoria came over holding my hand, she was thoroughly confused. Victoria simply replied, "well you looked so damn scared I thought you would pass out if I told you off ... so I decided to adopt you instead". We all shared a huge laugh as we reminisced about of our first meeting.

    I am brought out of my memory and into reality at the sight of another one of my friends, Alayna pulling up to the valet station; her car is inconspicuous, blending in with the scenery behind it. Alayna drove a grey Toyota Camry she got the day we graduated from college. The picture of ordinary, she stood 5'6 and heavier set, with sandy blond hair that she wore in whatever style nature decided that day. Today it is a mixture of frizzy curls and waves. I stare into her blue eyes and in that moment I appreciate her authenticity.

When Love Isn't Enough

It was her caring nature that brought us together. I remember the day I met Alayna like it was yesterday. I was walking through campus and being the klutz that I am, tripped over my own two feet walking to my dorm Sanford Hall. Of course my backpack was not closed all the way and all of my books fell on the ground. My cheeks flushed with embarrassment as I began to quickly gather my things hoping that none of the guys that lived next door had seen what happened, especially Darnell. Most people just looked at me continuing to walk by and some even snickered.

I felt the presence of someone kneeling next to me and helping me pick up my books. I looked up to see Alayna smiling a very warm smile at me as we picked up the last of the books on the floor. She handed me my books, released a soft giggle and told me to be more careful. "Hi, I'm Alayna" she said with an extended hand. "Arya" I managed nervously. "Pleased to meet you Arya", we shook hands and exchanged huge grins; the rest was history.

When Love Isn't Enough

I notice the girls are being escorted to a private section of the restaurant that was blocked off by beautiful French doors. I would be willing to bet every dime that I have this is the work of Desi or Tahj. Those two women could get VIP passes to the White House if they wanted too. My thoughts were redirected to my missing friend as I look around the room. Where the heck was Victoria? That girl is going to be late to her own funeral. I giggle rather loudly; hoping not to interrupt the people around me , I cup my mouth with my hand.

I decide to go over to the room where the girls are meeting and I walk in just in time to see everyone smiling and hugging; saying their hellos. Desi is the first one to ask a question; "Tahj how is work? I read in Business Weekly that you have taken on a major new client for NC power?" Tahj looks a little embarrassed, "actually I did; they asked me to head up the project last month and we have been keeping it under wraps. It's the biggest client I have taken on by myself since the promotion". Desi replies with a twinge of jealousy, "I envy you Tahj". Tahj chuckles and rolls her eyes... "You envy me? Desi you have everything anyone could ever want and more; you have: the dream husband who adores you, two beautiful children, a house to die for, you drive a different car every year and you take vacations whenever you want on your private jet. Oh and did I mention, you don't have to work? Do you really need me to continue with all of the reasons why *you* shouldn't envy *me*?" Desi laughs, "I guess you are right".

Alayna rolls her eyes, slightly annoyed by Desi's halfhearted compliment to Tahj and chimes in, "Tahj your life is nothing to snuff at! You are the youngest Executive Vice President in the history of the company. Your car selection isn't bad either and your penthouse downtown has an amazing view of the city; so stop your whining" Tahj chuckles, "Who's whining? I am just stating the fact that Desi has it made... So how's the job going for you Alayna?" Alayna sighs, "Being an administrative assistant was not the job that I had always dreamed of, but it pays the bills, so I won't complain too much". Alayna finishes her last thought as Victoria breezes by me, "I'm sorry I'm late, there was a ton of traffic".

She looks around and sees Tahj's face, which was contorted into a grimace. "Ok fine, my mother took *forever* to come and pick up the kids". This time she was slower to pick up her gaze and Desi was staring at her with an amused expression. With a sigh, Victoria began again, "What really happened was, I got out to the car and started it only to realize I had no gas! I had to stop for gas on the way"... she looks around in time to see Alayna roll her eyes. She pauses ... "I couldn't find my keys?" ... in unison Desi, Tahj and Alayna retorted "*Victoria*!!!"

She rolls her eyes, and with an exasperated sigh began with what was finally the truth..."Uh fine"... "My kids have been with my mom for the last two hours, my gas tank was filled up by Max last night, and I did not see a single car on my way here", she looks around and continues, "I sat on the toilet scrolling down my Facebook newsfeed and checking emails. I waited until the last minute to get ready so now I am thirty minutes late". Victoria couldn't even look up because she was so embarrassed, until she hears the girls' laugh.

Desi was the first to speak, "I knew your ass was on Facebook! I saw you sharing videos while I was at the restaurant waiting for you to get here". All the girls fell out laughing. I step out of the shadows and get ready to speak when the waitress walks in carrying a tray full of waters. She takes their drink orders and excuses herself. Alayna's next statement shoots through my bones like ice, "I wish Arya was here". Tahj replies, "I miss her so much every day, even after all this time". Victoria and Desi look at each other with tears in their eyes.

> "Death may indeed be final, but the love we share while living is eternal."
>
> -Don Williams Jr.

Chapter 2
The fallen Rose

At the thought of that last memory, they each instinctively reach for jewelry that they are wearing. Tahj reaches for her bracelet, Victoria her ring, Desi her earrings and Alayna her necklace. I walk over to the table to get a closer look and I immediately understand why. Each of them has on a piece of jewelry that exhibits a black rose. If I had tears they would be forming in my eyes as I look around the table. Their faces have various expressions of pain and anguish.

I look down at my own wrist and see the tattoo of a black rose vine that wraps the entirety of my arm and I think back to the day of that terrible accident; the day I lost my life. I think back to the day I saw that same pain and anguish on their faces as they were asked to identify my body. Desi was listed as my next of kin since I had no family here in the States; she got the call from the police when they came across the accident scene. She immediately called the girls and told them what happened to me and that the police said I didn't make it. They wanted to be there to support each other in case it was actually true.

I remember hearing them silently pray as they were escorted into the morgue asking God to let it be anyone but me. I remember the icy silence as the medical examiner unlocked the metal cooler and pulled out the slab. I remember ... nothing... for a long time nothing... and then I heard Desi say "okay" in a very soft voice... Then I remember out of the darkness, a blood curdling scream that pierced the air as Desi howled out in anguish. I remember Tahj falling to her knees and covering her eyes sobbing un-controllably. Victoria ran across the room and collapsed as she curled into a fetal ball and rocked back and forth. Alayna held my hand and screamed NO! NO! NO! …

When Love Isn't Enough

I shudder at the thought of that memory as I am dragged back into reality as Victoria breaks the silence, "I miss her so much that words cannot begin to express my pain. She was the one that brought us all together and the mystery of her death was what bonded us". I just sit, frozen like stone thinking back to my death and the mystery that clouded it. Even though it's painful every time the girls get together, I am just so overwhelmed with emotion that I have to be where they are. My strong presence in their hearts and minds brings me to their reality for a little while and when they leave I evaporate into nothingness.

The somber tone lingers for a few moments longer as memories of me flood their minds when the waitress returns with their drinks. She takes their orders and exits once more. At the sight of alcohol their eyes light up like children on Christmas Day. They are all delighted by this automatic response and they laugh hysterically immediately lightening the mood.

The rest of the dinner goes off without a hitch. Victoria tells the girls that her kids are coming back from a summer with grandma and they will be a welcome distraction, even though her husband is home the house is just a little too quiet. Tahj tells them all a little bit more about her newest client and that she was a little worried about whether or not she could handle it. All of the girls showed her support and in their own ways gave her encouragement.

Desi mentions how she was leaving for Orlando, Florida tomorrow to take the kids to Disney before school starts. She asks Victoria if she wants her to send the jet back when the girls come back from grandmas so they could join her in Disney. Victoria responds with an enthusiastic "yes" to which everyone chuckles. Desi and Victoria exchange flight details as Alayna tells the girls about the latest drama between her friends Antonio and Moe. Dinner moved on very quickly and it was time for dessert.

When Love Isn't Enough

Victoria reminds the girls that it was almost Tahj's 36th birthday to which Tahj sent her a warning glance; Victoria acknowledges with a smirk and continues her thought anyway. She tells the girls she has been trying to convince Tahj to go to the Dominican Republic for her birthday but she had refused. Desi and Alayna chime in that they think it was a great idea and she should go. Tahj ponders this thought for a moment; she asked Desi and Alayna if they want to go.

Alayna replies sadly that she wants to go but has no vacation time left with her job. Desi said that she would let her know once she checks with her husband. Victoria says "You already know I am there, just tell me when". Tahj replies, "I am not saying no... yet" and with a tone of finality the conversation progresses. After some protest from all of the girls, Tahj pays for dinner and the girls head to the Valet station and hand him their tickets. As their various cars pull up, they hug and say their goodbyes driving off into the sunset.

When Love Isn't Enough

    After they depart, their energy left with them, and like always, I disappear into nothingness, filled with warmth from the last meeting with my best girlfriends.

"If I was meant to be controlled, I would have come with a remote"

-Anonymous

Chapter 3
The Collar

```
Desi
```

    I spent all day slaving away in the kitchen. I fed the kids, made them their dinner and sent them upstairs to shower and get ready for bed. Their first day of school was tomorrow and Amy (my nanny) would be there early to get the kids. As the clock chimes to announce the passing of yet another hour Daniel was still not home. Earlier today after the kids and I came home from Disney, I did the laundry like always, to get Daniel and the kids ready for the upcoming week.

    As I was shaking out Daniels pockets and putting his pants in the wash, something red caught my eye. I picked up the shirt that had the red stain and I noticed a very distinct shade of *Whore Red* that I do not wear, smeared across my husband's collar. I sat there stunned and shocked in silence as I tried to process what I was seeing. I mean, did it really come as a shock to me to know that my husband was cheating? ... The honest answer to that question was no. I started to get the feeling that Daniel was sleeping around about a three months ago. He suddenly changed the passcode to his phone and started coming home later and later.

At first, he would call and tell me he was running late. Then it became a text, and then an email from his assistant; now... nothing. He originally told me it was due to a new major client he was taking on. Then it was an important meeting or a presentation that he had to work on. Now he just says he was working late and offers no explanation.

As the time rolled on and it was nearing 8:30 pm, I put his dinner in the warmer and head upstairs to put the children to bed and get their clothes ready for tomorrow. It was well past 9 o'clock after I had read stories, tucked them in and gave them good night kisses. I made up excuses as to the whereabouts of their father. I hated having to lie to my children. I made my way downstairs and I just knew he would be in the kitchen eating his dinner when I got there. When I rounded the corner to the kitchen it was just as empty as I had left it.

    I pour myself a glass of wine and walk to the laundry room to get the shirt off the dryer. I can't bring myself to wash it. I know it is risky to bring my discovery to my husband's attention because I do not want to leave him. I am not ready for that. As a woman I cannot ignore what he so blatantly put in my face. I try not to look at his phone because I was always told if you go looking for something you will find it. However, I didn't go looking for this. It came looking for me.

    I drink my wine, and pour myself glass after glass as I try to find the words I want to say to my husband; as the hours tick on. The next thing I know I hear tires rolling along the driveway and come to a stop outside the garage. By the time I hear the car door slam I had worked myself into quite a tizzy. I somehow muster a soft laugh as I hear him put the alarm on his car and turn the key in the lock on the front door. I sit silently as he walks into the kitchen, "What's for dinner?" he says as he opened to refrigerator and peered inside. I stare at him in complete disgust as I catch a whiff of a woman's perfume in the breeze when he walked by.

He didn't even glance in my direction to notice what I was holding in my hand or that I had finished an entire bottle of wine. My silence finally intrigued him enough for him to glance over his shoulder and see what I had in my hand for the first time. He glares at me, "Well Desi, are you going to answer me or are you going to just sit there looking stupid?" I start seeing red and in response to his question, I simply held up the shirt and wait for comprehension to wash over his face.

He looks unbothered as he closes the refrigerator door and turns to stare at me. "What the hell do you want Desi? I haven't got all night; I'm tired". I glare at him; my eyes were barely a slit now. "Would you care to explain to me why you have lipstick on your collar?" He just sighs and goes over to the wet bar, grabs a glass and pours himself a scotch. We sit in silence glaring at each other for what seems like an eternity.

He finally broke the silence with a firm "No". I said "excuse me?" He took a sip of his drink and said, "No ... I would not care to explain to you why I have lipstick on my collar" followed by another sip of his drink. My mouth drops, *why was he talking to me this way? As if I was nothing.* I try as quickly as I can to refocus my thoughts. Calmly I continue, "I found this in the laundry, I've noticed that you are coming home later and later, and you seem like a different person lately. I'm not a fool so I know something is going on and I want to know what it is". He sips his drink again (that little move was starting to get under my skin) and took his sweet time answering the question.

     Finally, he looks at me with a look of disdain and says "What do you want to know?" I reply with a simple "Everything". He pauses very slightly, almost as if contemplating his next move in a chess match. He walks slowly over to me grabs the shirt as if he were going to examine it. He takes a lighter out of his pocket, put the shirt in the trash can and set it on fire. The flames dance around my vision as if doing an eerie and disturbing ritual. I glance at my husband with shock drenching my face. *Who was this man?* I knew I needed to put out the flames but my feet had turned to lead and I was unable to move.

     After about thirty seconds, he slowly reaches under the sink and pulls out the fire extinguisher. He pulls out the pin, grabs the handle and sweeps it from side to side until there was nothing left but smoldering ashes. He moves his hair out of his face and looks at me with the eyes of someone who has nothing to lose. I am frightened in that moment; more frightened than I had ever been in my life.

He picks up his glass from the counter and takes another sip. He looks at me and says, "Well it's obvious isn't it?" His response startles me because after his latest episode I cannot think clearly anymore. All I can get out of mouth, through the foggy haze that had consumed my brain was "what?" He replies condescendingly, "You asked me what I was doing. You wanted to know everything... I am asking you... Isn't it obvious what I am doing? You used to be such a smart girl Desi". I just stare at him shocked by the sarcasm that hung on his every word and all I could get out was an exasperated "Excuse me?" I had been prepared for a few tears and a heartfelt apology, with a promise of change. I was not prepared for this!

He continued as if talking to a small child, "Well clearly, you already know what I have been doing Desdemona. So why are we having this conversation. Why would you even ask?" At this point my blood starts to boil. "You are going to stop doing this now Daniel! Or else..."

He sips that damn drink again and laughs an almost sinister laugh, "Or else what Desdemona? You're going to leave? You are going to give up this lifestyle that your spoiled ass has gotten accustomed to? You are going to give up your $200,000 dollar car, your 5,000 handbags, and put your children into public schools? Get real Desi. What will you do with yourself? *Nothing*, you were nothing before me and you will be nothing after me. I will make sure of it".

I have the perfect response in my mind; that I was something before him. I was successful and climbing the corporate ladder and the only reason I stopped working was because he did not want someone else raising our children. I was still so shocked that I could not force my lips to move, so I sit here in silence.

When Love Isn't Enough

My eyes follow him as he moves to exit the room and pauses at the door, turning to face me "Now, I am going to go take a shower since you are done wasting my time. You are really starting to give me a headache and I don't want to hear about this again." My mind had finally caught up with the situation and I scream as loudly as I can, "I don't have to take this shit I am out of here!"

I walk across the kitchen where he had stopped in the doorway and brush past him on my way to the living room." "Where the hell do you think you are going?" he yells. "I am going to get my children and I am leaving you", I retort. Before I can even register what is happening he grabs my wrist whips me around and my face meets his fist.

"A House Where A Woman Is Unsafe Is Not A Home"

-Woman, Liberia

Chapter 4

Pain

My husband grabs me by the hair and throws me up against the wall. Repeatedly punching and kicking me. He leans over my body as I lay there bleeding and broken. He says "How dare you have the nerve... No the audacity to question me about where I am and who I'm seeing? I take care of you. You have no right to ask me anything. "

"You sick bastard. I can check whatever the fuck I want to, because I am your wife and you don't get to step out on me because I am worth more than that." Well that's what I want to say to him. You see, he has one unfair advantage in this relationship and that is he is extremely wealthy. Before I met my husband I was very independent. I had my Master's Degree from Berkeley and I was on my way to doing amazing things as I climbed the corporate

When Love Isn't Enough

ladder at my fortune 500 company. Then I met my husband and he wooed me, and knocked me off my feet. He gave me five of the best years, two beautiful children, a wonderful home, and trips whenever I wanted to take them with a private jet at my disposal. Unfortunately, the one thing I had to do was sell my soul.

I sold my soul to a man who didn't respect me; who didn't love me, and the idea of leaving him terrified me. He not only could take away my livelihood - but he also had the means and the resources to take away my children; my two beautiful children that I can't live without.

So as I lay here on this floor, broken, battered and bruised – that strong voice inside of me that wanted to lash out at that son of a bitch for what he is doing to me... silently weeps and creeping back inside of me until it was just a tremble.

I am left here with my thoughts (as he punches me, kicks me, and pulls my hair) as to how I got here. *Desi, how did you let yourself get here? You were so strong (The voice in my head begins to crack),* everybody looked up to you, and they saw great things. You were voted most likely to succeed. How did I get here? At what point did this man turn on me and I just didn't see it? It's never been this bad before. It's never been this violent before. There were signs, but was I just too smitten to see them? Was I too wrapped up in my wonderful lifestyle to see them?

    You see it's my fault. I blame myself because I knew he was creeping. I knew he was stepping out and has been for a while now. I don't know exactly when it started, but I let him. I let him because there was a certain lifestyle that I always envisioned for myself... that I needed. I let him because he paid my mother's rent. I let him because I have always been told to stay in my place as a woman and submit to my husband. I let him even though I knew it was wrong. And now... where do I stand?

"Remember… No one is a failure that has friends"

-It's a wonderful Life

Chapter 5

Friend Zone

Alayna

I walk past my neighbor who has a smug look on her face, arm in arm with Antonio. I chuckle to myself knowing what this must look like to her. Antonio is one of the most handsome men I have ever met. He stands 6'4 and has a body build like the Gods. A football player for the Carolina Panthers, he is definitely impressive eye candy. Yet, he's walking arm in arm with me; a very plain looking woman. He looked down at me with his almond shaped eyes inquisitively; he must've heard me laugh. I stare at him "oh, it's nothing"; he accepts my response and walks me to my door.

His phone rings, he looks at it and answers without skipping a beat, "Hey love. No, I'm not doing anything just dropping off Alayna. Okay see you soon baby". He gives me a hug and a kiss on the forehead; with a promise to see me soon, he turns around and walks away. Ugh, I hate when he does that. He takes me out for a perfectly wonderful evening and then prances off into the sunset to be with his model girlfriend.

It's always like that though. To an outsider, like my nosy neighbor, it must look like I live a fabulous life. I have some really amazing and handsome male friends that come and go at all times of the night. They are always affectionate to me and they all love me. The truth is that I am the administrative assistant for an attorney that represents a lot of important men throughout the city. I have never been easily intimidated or easily impressed by anyone; that allows me to just be my goofy, carefree, and nerdy self. Men that walk into my office are accustomed to women fawning over them and they find my genuine nature very refreshing. The problem is that they never see me as more than that; the refreshingly human friend that happens to be a woman.

When Love Isn't Enough

    I change into my pajamas and heat up a frozen dinner; grab a glass of wine, and plop down on the couch in front of the TV. I mindlessly flip through the channels and reflect back to my lunch with the girls yesterday. I feel a pang of jealously rush through me and it causes my stomach to ache. I immediately regret the feeling of jealousy coursing through my veins but I cannot force it to leave my body. So I am left with the thoughts that cause this reaction.

    Why am I so jealous? Hhhmmm lets see... Seeing my friends drive off in their ridiculously expensive cars as I hop into my ten year old Camry. I mean seriously, the friend that is the closest to me on the "normal" scale is Victoria; and even she drives an Acura truck. Or maybe, it's knowing that they are driving home to their ridiculously lavish homes as I come home to this apartment that I can barely afford. Maybe it's the fact that they are all drop dead gorgeous with amazing bodies (including the two that have children) and me – well I am cute enough but my body is shapeless and leaves a lot to be desired.

    I mean, I can't really complain about my life (even though I often find a reason to). I have a car to get me back and forth to work and I have a stable job that doesn't give me much else but it allows me to pay the bills (even if sometimes it is barely). I have great friends and I am rarely alone. I not only have my girlfriends but I also have a great group of guy friends that I hang out with on the regular. However, my love life is as dry as the Sahara! I haven't even had to pull out my sexy underwear in over a year.

    I shouldn't really complain... It's just that I envisioned so much more for myself. I had so many dreams and high hopes for what my life would be after college. My friends found great jobs right away and I kind of stumbled along doing various temp jobs for about six months; my student loans kicked in and I had to take the first stable job that I could find to try to pay them, and I have been there ever since.

When Love Isn't Enough

  I wanted to buy a new car for a while now but I am so saddled with debt and collections that I can't afford one if I wanted to. Even if I could afford one my credit is so bad that they would laugh me out of the dealership. If I did happen to qualify for financing they would charge me some ridiculous interest rate that would make the payment unaffordable anyway, and I would be back at square one. So for now, I will just go on a wing and a prayer that old Bessie will make it until I can afford a new car.

  I realize that I have a frown on my face, causing wrinkles on my forehead as I think about my life. I know I should do something about my situation if I am that unhappy but I am just too afraid to make a change. I have gotten so used to being normal that I don't know how to be anything else anymore. I get up and grab my dinner out of the microwave and walk back over to the couch. I sip my wine and start to flip through the channels.

When Love Isn't Enough

My phone buzzes near my feet that are propped up on the couch - in my favorite fuzzy socks. I stare at the penguins on my feet and they make me smile. I grab my phone and see Moe pop up on my notification panel. I swipe the phone and read the text that says, *I'm bored and on my way to your place so wake your ass up and let me in.* I literally laugh out loud and reply, "How do you know I don't have a hot date?"... The bubble pops up on my IPhone letting me know that he is writing me back.

I frown as his message pops up on the screen *Haha, Very funny. Now come answer the damn door I am here.* I wanted to be angry but I knew he was right. He didn't need to announce his arrival because there was no hot date to be had. I sigh, drag myself off of the couch and open the door. In front of me was a handsome olive skinned man in a silk button up shirt that draped comfortably over his small frame, "Hey Moe" I smile. "Hey", he says as he brushes past me and plops on the couch. He then grabs my glass of wine and takes a huge sip. "What are we watching? Oh and this is good by the way! You might want to grab yourself some more wine while you grab us a snack! I will sit here, drinking my new found glass of wine and find something to watch on TV". I pick up the closest pillow I can get my hands on and throw it at the back of his head. *Bullseye*! He chuckles grabbing the back of his head. I walk into the kitchen to grab us a snack and myself a new glass of wine.

When Love Isn't Enough

"There are some people so poor that the only thing they have is money."

-www.livelifehappy.com

Chapter 6
Money and Happiness

Tahj

Today started out just like any other day. I get up at 4:30, read my emails so I can try to get a head start on my day. I go into my beautiful kitchen – in my large penthouse, make myself a cup of coffee and grab a granola bar and head out to the balcony. It's a beautiful sunrise over Charlotte, NC and I watch the sun pass over the Bank of America stadium. I think about how amazing my life is. That thought is short lived as one of my many alarms goes off.

I have my morning routine laid out so precisely that every time I need to make progress an alarm goes off alerting me. That particular alarm tells me it is time for me to jump in the shower. I go to my bathroom which has the most beautiful Italian marble and heated floors. I take off my robe and hang it on the door. I look at myself in the mirror at my perfect body. I have breasts that are perky and a perfect D cup. My stomach is flat with a hole in my belly button where my belly button ring used to be. My legs are beautifully toned from all of the running I do. I turn my body slightly to the side to catch a side view. I have always loved my butt. It is one of my favorite things on my body.

As I admire the perfect roundness of my behind, I hum along to E-40's line "her booty's bigger than a Prius" and I grin. Then I notice a dimple on my butt cheek in the mirror; *Oh hell no*! I have to tell my trainer about that when I see him next. I am pulled out of a trance by another alarm going off. That was my alarm telling me to get out of the mirror or off the toilet and actually get in the shower.

I laugh at how well I know myself and turn on the water until steam fills up the bathroom. I get into the shower and just as I start to get a good lather going my next alarm goes off. That is extremely annoying and I did not have enough time. I think I will have to shave off a few minutes of my wasting time after breakfast alarm and add it to my shower time. I get lost in thought rinsing the water off my body; my "stop wasting time complaining" alarm goes off.

    I sigh and step out of the shower. I brush my teeth and remove my scarf from my hair. My hair is perfect as usual as I undo my rollers. I step into my room which automatically heated up five degrees when I turned on the shower - so that it is not cold when I get out. I walk into my huge walk in closet and decide what I am going to wear today.

    I grab the closest dress to me that I haven't even removed the tag from and a blazer hanging next to it. I open the drawer and grab some underwear (to which I notice it is all the same... black or white and comfortable). I sigh and close the door and go to the middle island and grab some pearl earrings and a necklace. I put on my black rose bracelet that I wear every day and walk over to my makeup area and slide on my underwear. I do my makeup and put on the rest of my jewelry, and as I am slipping on my dress my alarm goes off alerting me that I need to leave in five minutes.

    I throw on my jacket and go over to my rotating shoe rack. As it spins around my thoughts wander aimlessly about what I have to do within my first hour at the office. I spot the shoes that I want and throw them onto my feet. I grab my purse and briefcase and head out of the door. Before my car is thoroughly warmed up I am on my first conference call that starts at 7. I pull up to the front of my office building and head under the building into the parking garage. I don't have to drive very far because my spot is one of the first reserved spots in the structure. I get out of my car, press the alarm, and head to the elevator of the parking garage.

I go up to the main lobby and walk across a very grand room with beige and gold marble lining the floors and walls. The foyer has high ceilings and a wall of floor to ceiling windows. I walk over to the security area and the guard hands me my coffee. She is the sweetest woman that I know. I smile, nod and mouth the words thank you; to which she replies with a huge grin.

I scan my badge and walk towards the elevator. Almost as if on cue, the conference call ended as the elevator doors open. My morning routine was as beautifully choreographed as the waltz. I take the elevator to the 40th floor; the second from the top. I make my way to my corner office and I notice the girls in my office gawking at me as I walk by; whispering amongst themselves. My office is on the far end of the floor. As I near my office door, I walk past my assistant that hands me a list of memos and my schedule for the day.

When Love Isn't Enough

      I groan as I notice that an emergency conference call has been scheduled over my lunch break. My assistant looks at me with understanding in his eyes as I walk into my office. My office is impressive enough on its own. It is huge, with marble floors and a large cherry oak desk, located slightly to the left; that takes up half of the room. There is a glass bookcase that lines the far wall that is filled with business books as well as some of my personal favorites. What sets my office apart is that one of the walls is covered with floor to ceiling windows; which gives me a perfect view of the city skyline. I walk over to my desk, put down my bags and turn on my computer.

      As my computer whirs to life I think about how I must look to those girls that were looking at me in the office. I walked past them in my $500 shoes, $4000 handbag, fresh manicure, pedicure and hairstyle all from the night before. I have a briefcase that costs more than their rent. They see my expensive car and my two cell phones. One phone is always hooked up to my blue tooth and the other always in my hand as I look at my emails.

I must look completely put together. I hear them whispering how they wish they could be me. How I have everything. I smirk at that thought as I get logged onto my computer and pull up my notes as I get ready for my next conference call which is only the beginning of a string of conference calls that makes up every Monday. I feel lost and completely un-accomplished, in spite of everything that I have done in my life.

The amazing part is that I have done more than most women who are thirty-five have even dreamed of doing. I climbed the corporate ladder so fast; all I did was kept my nose in the books, worked long hours, and kept my head to the ground. While everyone else was out having a good time, I was working. I studied and worked my ass off, making it to the top. Yet, I lost something in the meantime; I lost me.

I had never really taken the time to stop and date. I mean I met guys and they

When Love Isn't Enough

were nice and all but they were never up to my standards. I think I set the bar so high after I tried that whole dating thing once right out of college. I married my college sweetheart. He left me... *he left me*... He told me that I had nothing going for me and that I had no future; that I was weighing him down. He left me... We are not even going to get into the story of how he left me, which is a story for another day.

After that I didn't have time for anything or anybody because my objective was to prove him wrong. I passed that sorry SOB a long time ago. I never stopped and now here I stand on the eve of my 36th birthday and I feel completely lost and alone. I haven't taken time to do anything outside of work. You know its funny how you get on the other side of thirty and you start to have some revelations. It happened to me before in my 20's but it wasn't nearly as bad. Even then I felt I wasn't young anymore. I had already been married, divorced, and I had a chip on my shoulder.

This feels different; I am on my way to forty and I have nothing outside of work to show for it and no one here to share in my success with me. My parents died a few years back and I have a younger brother but he's doing his own thing across the country. We used to try to get together for holidays but recently we haven't even done that. So it's just me. Thank God I have my girlfriends to keep me company because I don't know what I would do without them. They keep me grounded and give me the strength to push forward. I am really evaluating my life at the moment and I feel like I am going through some sort of weird midlife crisis that I don't understand.

As I sit here in my "perfect life", envied by so many, I feel as alone as I have ever felt. Something has got to change. I was originally opposed to the idea of going on this trip with Victoria for my birthday and I blew her off; but I think I am going to take her up on it. She wants to go to the Dominican Republic but I have something else in mind. I have always wanted to go to

When Love Isn't Enough

Puerto Rico and I think I will go; because at this point I feel like I am going to end up alone.

    I have no husband or no prospect of one. Every man that I have dated has either been full of shit or married but I haven't really cared before because I never wanted anything serious with them. I have no children and that hurts the most. I have always wanted to be a mom but I lost sight of that.

    I am going to go on this trip and invite all of the girls. I call Tom into my office and ask him to check my schedule next week and tell me when I have a meeting that I cannot miss or re-schedule. He looks at me confused but obliges my request. He pulls out his IPad and runs his finger over the screen. "There are some things that will be difficult to move on Monday but other than that you are clear until Thursday. He looks up over his IPad and waits.

"Tom you said difficult, but not impossible... right?" He smirks at me and replies "Right... I am a miracle worker". I grin "well go work me some miracles, and book me a private jet to Puerto Rico leaving Saturday and coming back Tuesday, as well as travel arrangements". I thought I may need a day after my vacation to recuperate and catch up on some work.

Tom's eyes lit up in an almost mischievous way, "Yes ma'am" he replied with a rebellious laugh and with that he was off to spend the next two hours re-arranging my schedule and booking my reservations. He rolled his chair into my office grinning "So how many people are going?" I am not sure yet so book everything for three. This really confused him (If I had booked the reservations for two he could have assumed that I was going with a man). He frowns "okay" as he slides back out of my office to his desk.

I laughed silently to myself because I know he wants to know what all of this is

When Love Isn't Enough

about, but is too professional to ask... That was fine with me. I sent a text to the girls to invite them on the trip and my mind starts to wander to the things that I want in my life, but don't have yet. In that moment, I make a promise to myself, no matter what happens on this trip, I will have a good time and be open to the possibility of anything that may happen.

"Dear God. Thanks for this beautiful life and forgive me if sometimes it seems as if I don't love it enough"

-Anonymous

Chapter 7
A Tale As Old As Time

Victoria

A Tale as old as time; boy meets girl while they are in college. They graduate. The next year they are married. Boy and girl start great careers. Boy and girl buy a house. Then two years later they have a baby and then two years later another. Everything is picture perfect. A tale as old as time; but what happens when that's no longer enough?

You see that girl over there? That's me. I should be happy right? I have everything: A great husband, a wonderful house, beautiful children; I have it all. But deep down I am holding in a secret. I don't know how much longer I can take it and I don't know who to turn to. I don't even know how to begin to describe my unhappiness. I spent a lot of time growing up in relationships where I loved men way more than they loved me. I have been cheated on too many times to count. I have shed enough tears to fill an entire river.

I remember when I met my husband I was at my breaking point and I could not take another heartache. I prayed to God to bring me a man that would be predictable. That would never hurt me. To send me a man that loved me more than I loved him so I could never be hurt.

India Arie's song *I am Ready For Love* became my theme song. Chaka Khan's *Keep Your Head Up* became my anthem. I was about ready to give up on love when I went to a Kappa party on campus to kick off the start of senior year. The Kappa's strolled around the party doing their signature "shimmy" and I saw a man through the crowd. He was absolutely handsome. He came over to me in his red jacket; holding his cane. He told me I was the most beautiful girl he had ever seen and that I was his dream woman. He reached out his

When Love Isn't Enough

hand and told me his name, "Max". I blushed as I introduced myself, "Victoria". *Boy meets girl.*

We dated for the rest of our senior year and graduated together. He met my parents at Graduation; they loved him. To be honest, I did not feel like he was the one at that time, but he was nicer to me than any other man had ever been; so I stuck it out. He was so un-exciting that I was comforted by his predictability. When he met the rest of my family and they loved him, I started to fall for him. *Boy and girl fall in love.* We were married shortly after college and bought a house as our gift to each other. *Boy and girl buy a house.*

I started working in a marketing firm based on a recommendation that I got through my friend Desi. She had a job there and referred me. I started out as an unpaid intern but I quickly climbed the corporate ladder. My husband started working in Retail after college and was quickly promoted to a store manager. Our hours were a little crazy but we made it work. *Boy and girl get good jobs.*

My husband never really wanted kids but it was always something that I wanted especially after being told that I might not be able to have them. We got pregnant and we lost that baby for unexplained reasons three months into my pregnancy. We got pregnant again shortly after that and had my first daughter Natalia. We were overjoyed and decided to try to have our next child close to her so that they could grow up together. We got pregnant again and could not have been happier.

Unfortunately, that pregnancy ended up being ectopic. I was devastated and I almost lost my life on the operating table. We decided that we were not going to have any more children because we could not deal with the devastation that followed a pregnancy loss again. Wouldn't you know that God had other plans as I got pregnant with my second daughter Hazel while on birth control.

When Love Isn't Enough

With the birth of my second daughter my family was complete. *A tale as old as time.* My husband and I have been though a lot together in our nine years of marriage. We went through the death of his father and the losses of our children and we got each other through it all. My life was perfect and it should have been smooth sailing from here on out... right?

Wrong. I always felt like I was on cruise control throughout my life. Every day was the same: get up earlier than everyone in the house, get the kids clothes laid out, make the kids their breakfast, wake the kids up, fight with them to get out of bed, pack the kids lunch and pack my husband's lunch. Kiss my husband goodbye, drop the kids off at school, go to work, leave work, pick the kids up from the sitter, make dinner, do homework with the kids, fight with them to get their showers, get into bed, read a bedtime story, talk to husband about our days, clean, have a glass of wine (or three), read a chapter or two of my book, be in bed by ten and wake up the next morning; Repeat.

There is nothing *wrong* with my life but it's just not what I thought I was signing up for. I expected date nights under the stars with my husband and kids that came with an instruction manual. My parents didn't make it look this hard. My husband once said to me, on a well-deserved vacation away from the kids, that I was not fun anymore. I was so annoyed and wanted to scream, "*I was a shit ton of fun before I started dating you*! Nights out in the club: drinking, dancing and having lots of sex!" I smiled. We only have sex once a week if that, and to be honest it's not very good. My body no longer felt alive and I don't feel butterflies anymore when he touches me and I often find myself letting my mind wander to other things during sex (like what I have to do tomorrow); I am not the girl that I once was.

I sit here wallowing in self-pity when my text message alert goes off; it's a message

When Love Isn't Enough

from Tahj. I swipe my phone open and I see that she has decided she actually wants to go on the trip. My heart literally smiles! She has changed the destination but *who cares*? I am just so freaking excited for an excuse to get away from this hum drum life that I reply to her text with an all caps "YES"!

    I jump out of my chair, sprint up the stairs and whip out my suitcase. I dig deep into my closet to see if I still have some of my sexy clothes from college. I pray as I try on some of the outfits, but they still fit even though I have filled out a little more in the butt and breast region. I just need a new swimsuit and heels which I will buy tomorrow. I continue to pack for an hour before I realize that I haven't even told my husband I was leaving. I guess I should do that, I think to myself as I sprint out of my room. This trip will be exactly what I need!

> *"We'll be friends until we are old and senile... Then we will be new friends."*
>
> -Anonymous

Chapter 8

Feel the Energy

```
Tahj
```

I board the jet and fully expect to have to wait for Victoria because she is *always* late. Imagine my surprise when I board the plane and she is sitting there with a drink already in her hand. I laugh hysterically at the sight of her and she just rolls her eyes and chuckles, with immediate understanding. "Somebody is excited for this trip! I have honestly never seen you so excited or *early* in my life" I manage to get out through laughter. She rolls her eyes but nods in agreement, telling me that she couldn't wait to get away. I paused perplexed by the tone in her voice when she made that statement; I feel like there is more behind her words, but I decide that now is not the time to pry.

I tell Victoria I need to do some work on the plane so that I can enjoy myself when we land. She tells me that she understands and also needs some time to get her "thoughts together" before we land. They seal the door on the plane and the flight attendant walks up to me with a fresh Mimosa; I can get used to this. An uneventful three hours later, we land in Puerto Rico's airport.

Within an hour we have our bags and we're walking over to the counter for the transportation that we had previously ordered. We sit outside of the airport waiting for the shuttle to take us to the Barceló - the hotel where we were staying - and I think to myself, it is hot as hell! Now don't get me wrong, Charlotte gets hot but not with this kind of humidity.

I look around cursing this damn heat and I noticed that the men were absolutely gorgeous; many of them stop what they are doing to smile at me. I smile back at them and say in almost a whisper to Victoria, "I think that I am going to like it here". I look over and notice Victoria peering over the top of her sunglasses at the obvious man candy and laugh. She meets my gaze and gives me that look that only best girlfriends can understand; the look that says "GGGIIIRRRRLLLLLL". We both giggle and at that moment our shuttle pulls up.

Our driver, an older man that in his prime would have been quite the charmer, put our bags into the back of the shuttle and grabs our hands helping us inside. He tells us about Puerto Rican culture and landmarks as we rode to our hotel. I didn't speak a lick of Spanish so I will be relying a lot on Victoria, who was fluent.

As we make our way through the city I notice a lot of abandoned and run down areas. I am a little disappointed because I expected to be in a tropical paradise. We pull up to our hotel, which is protected by a gated entry and an armed guard; which made me a little nervous. Once we make it through the gate we take the long drive to our hotel. We neared the hotel, it's starting to look more and more like the paradise I had envisioned. I might not have to fire Tom after all. I giggle to myself and catch Victoria's inquisitive gaze. In response I just shake my head and she shrugs turning her head back towards the window, I do the same.

We pull up to the largest hotel that I have ever seen. The main building is the color of the pure white sandstone and stood a massive seventy-five feet tall; as I looked out behind it I see at least a half-dozen other buildings; all smaller than the first, but still equally impressive. The ceilings are very high and have leaves attached to a ceiling fan that spun around creating the faintest breeze in the lobby. This place is amazing; I can tell by Victoria's face that she was just as in awe as I am.

We are greeted by the bellman that takes our bags and tells us there is no need for us to check in because that had already been taken care of. In that moment I think to myself, I need to give Tom a raise. He informs us that we will be staying in a suite off the water. I try not to look too impressed but inside I was like a giddy school girl. Victoria doesn't maintain her composure as well as I do; she rather loudly says "Girl you hooked it up! This is beautiful".

We walk through the hotel noticing all of the shops and restaurants that line the halls. We also notice several bars and even a casino, we decide that we will visit these places later. We walk outside of the main building and end up on a path along the beach that is lined with large palm trees. This hotel is much bigger than I originally thought. There are three pools, including one that looks like it has a pool bar; I make a note to myself to check that out. There are multiple buildings that look like they house about one-hundred rooms each.

We finally arrive at the building nearest the water and make our way to one of the corner rooms. The bellman opens the door for us and holds it open so that we could enter. The room was huge! We enter the suite to a large living area with a sixty-inch flat screen TV. The colors in the room are very neutral, but work with the feng shui of the island. The couch is a seafoam green with brown and white throw pillows and the floor a tan tile that glistened slightly in the light. To the right there is a small kitchen that has maple colored cabinets, dark granite counters and stainless steel appliances.

I looked to the left and notice a bedroom. Victoria and I walk in, look at each other and gape. It is beautiful, it has a large King sized bed and fluffy white comforters. The walls and ceiling are white, with a green accent wall and the décor is reminiscent of the island. There is a bathroom on the right with stones lining the inside of the shower and brown tiles on the floor. The shower is large and encased in glass, with a rainfall shower head and body jets; it is spectacular even by my standards.

We walk out of the bathroom and Victoria runs past me and jumps on the bed exclaiming "mines!"... Before I can open my mouth to protest, the bellman, who clearly catches the look on my face, informs me that the other bedroom is identical to this one. I grin and thank him; secretly thinking that I need to tip him $50 for helping to avoid WW3 in this room.

He brings our bags to our bedrooms, we both tip him and then he leaves. We agree to shower and get dressed for our dinner reservations (Tom thought of everything), and then head to the bar. After a very nice dinner we go to one of the bars. Just like everywhere else in this place, all of the guys were incredibly cute. I make a note to myself that I will have to make this an annual trip.

The guys knew how to make you feel right at home. In the various versions of "*Morena*" and "*Bella*" being thrown our way, I ask Victoria what it means and she says that it means in layman's terms, beautiful.

We have an amazing time as the guys fight for our attention, doing anything to make us smile. I am really enjoying myself, although, I am not really taking the guys too seriously because they all seem like major flirts. There was one bartender that seems different. He came over to me and hands me a napkin with a heart on it. He tells me to hold his Corazon (heart) for him; I giggle at his cheesy gesture, but appreciate the originality and ask him for his name, "Juan" he says with a smile.

    Juan made sure that I had my drink filled the rest of the night. Victoria enjoyed the attention so much (a little too much) that she did not notice the subtle exchanges between Juan and I. We shut down the bar and Victoria wanted to go to the all night bar. I couldn't help my responsible side that informed her we had an early morning excursion. With a groan, she grudgingly agreed and we started to walk to our room. With a parting glance and smile, I left Juan at the bar wondering what tonight could have been.

A friend is one that knows you as you are, understands where you have been, accepts what you have become, and still, gently allows you to grow.

-William Shakespeare

Chapter 9
The Confession

Victoria

As we make our way back to the room I realize how much fun I had. I do not want tonight to end. If there was not the promise of us being here tomorrow, I don't think I could stand the idea of ending the night. I notice that Tahj has a smirk on her face the whole walk back to the room. Initially, she denies there was a cause for her light mood, and then she informs me about Juan. The whole time she talks my smile gets wider, until my face is twisted with Grinch like happiness (you know the look... after he ruined everybody's Christmas).

After various renditions of Tahj and Juan sitting in a tree and many death stares, we make it back to the room. We change into our pajamas and decide we will have a sleepover like we used to growing up. Tahj has been my best friend since we were children and she is more like my sister than my friend. Tahj makes her way into my room with a bottle of rum that we bought at the airport.

We sit on the bed and make small talk; I feel the truth bubbling up inside of me like bad liquor. I can't think of the right words, so I just blurt it out. "I want a divorce". The words stung like venom as they came out of my mouth. I am so embarrassed that I don't even want to look up. We sit in silence for what seems like an eternity. Tahj finally spoke very calmly, "Are you sure?" I look up with tears in my eyes... "Yes"... "Maybe"... "I don't know".

I proceed to explain to her the revelation I had just days earlier. She pauses, as she ponders everything that I tell her and then speaks calmly again. "Well, I can't say that I am surprised. I always wondered how long your marriage was going to last." My jaw drops and I shoot her an accusatory glance, "What do you mean?

When Love Isn't Enough

You knew my marriage was going to fail and you didn't tell me?" She continues, "Well it's just that you are such a vibrant and lively person and I have watched your happiness fade over the years. I have watched you fade into a person that I barely recognize and there is nothing wrong with that. You have responsibilities; as long as you were happy then I was happy". "But watching you tonight I knew that you were no longer happy".

I start to cry because as much as I hate to admit it everything that she said was true. I hate the person that I have become. Existing but not living; liking but not loving. I am so confused because I have always thought I was perfectly happy. Now, I am left to wonder if what I thought I felt was true happiness; or just happiness from not being hurt. I didn't even know that there was a difference until now.

I wasn't sure if I had changed or we both did; but somewhere along the way, something changed between my husband

and me. I just couldn't put my finger on it. As guilt washed over me, my shame began to consume me. I quietly weep and Tahj slides across the bed holding me in her arms. She hugs me and rubs my hair, telling me that everything is going to be alright. "I love you Victoria and I will support you no matter what", with that I drift off to sleep.

When Love Isn't Enough

"Passion is oxygen of the soul"

-Bill Butler

Chapter 10

You Just Show Up At My Door

Alayna

I step out of the shower massaging the kinks out of my neck, grab the towel off the hook next to the shower and wrap it around my body. I brush my teeth, wash my face and make my way into the bedroom. Sitting on the ottoman at the foot of my bed I put lotion on my legs and torso. As I lotion my body I ponder the predicament that I am in. I've spent a lot of time lonely; always surrounded by gorgeous men; but still lonely. How can you never be alone, but still be lonely?

I am left to wonder why? Why do they not find me attractive? Is it because I am overweight? Is it because I am too plain? Is it because I am the good girl? Or is it simply because they see me as one of the boys? ... I must admit that I am not very exciting compared to other women; I am not very spontaneous and I don't lead an exciting life; However, I am a good woman and I deserve to be happy.

Why do all of these: awful, gold digging, materialistic and cold hearted women, always finish first? It really is not fair! But then I look up at my reflection in the mirror… and I realize that I am a little bit less than beautiful at the moment. I sigh as I open the towel revealing the stretch marks that have formed around my belly button and lightly dance across my breasts; I am instantly reminded of why I am alone. I fit no man's standard of beautiful.

Every time I turn on the TV or open a magazine I see beautiful women with flawless skin and the perfect body. I even think of my friends who are all absolutely gorgeous. How am I supposed to compete out there in a world like that? I am constantly surrounded by Facebook posts and movies that tell me that because I am overweight I should be unhappy with myself, and I should feel ashamed. I didn't used to believe it; but now as I sit here rounding out my 34th year on this planet and I am still alone; I am forced to think that maybe everyone is right.

I reflect on the girls that date some of my best guy friends and how gorgeous and perfect they are. Being friends with a lot of powerful and attractive men, I see some beautiful women go through that revolving door. I look at myself one more time and sigh. I am so tired of always being second best and feeling less than; feeling average.

In that moment my doorbell rings. It is well past 10 o'clock so I look at my phone to see if I have any missed calls or messages that would explain my unexpected visitor... nothing... I grab the statue off the mantle and turn it upside down to form a weapon. If someone tries to come in this apartment today they have another thing coming.

I look through the peep hole and I see Antonio standing there covering his face; he looks completely broken. Without even thinking I put the statue down and I whip the door open. This man... this 6'4 perfectly built man is standing in my doorway; looking like a five year old child... broken.... crying. I think the worst; I think who just died?

Without even giving me so much as a hello he looks into my eyes and completely collapses onto my body. The sheer mass of his frame pushes me back into the apartment under the pressure; edging me out of the door frame. I guide him over to the couch and sit him down. I tell him that I will be right back. I rush over to the door, to close and lock it; Then, I run into the kitchen and secure a napkin. I hurry back to the couch and wipe away his tears; "What's wrong sweetheart? Tell me what's wrong". All he can get out between sobs is "She left me"; my mind becomes a blur, because his words don't make sense. Is he talking about his girlfriend?

They have been together for two years. He loves her to pieces and I thought she loved him back. She is one of those perfect girls that I was thinking about earlier. It doesn't make sense because they seem so happy. "She left me..." he mumbles again. "I feel like the wind has been knocked from beneath my sails" he cries. I reply, "Its ok sweetheart. Just tell me what happened".

Once he can control his sobs enough to speak he begins, "I came home after practice like I do every day and I saw that her bags were packed at the foot of the stairs. She came down the stairs and told me that she was not in love with me anymore. She said that she had found somebody else. I pleaded for her to reconsider and she laughed in my face and told me that her decision was already made. The doorbell rang and a guy was standing at the door; she gave him her bags."

He looks at me with eyes full of tears, but continues "I just stood there too shocked to move or speak; she grabbed my face, pulled my head down and gave me a kiss on the forehead. She told me that it had been fun, and for me to take care of myself as she walked out the door." I just stare at him with tears in my eyes. After a moment he took a deep breath, and began again, "When I finally regained control of my limbs, I drove around for hours not really knowing where I was going. Then when I came out of what felt like a trance, I was at your door".

    I was frozen and did not have any words to respond. He breaks down, consumed by his own thoughts. This time he cries into my shoulder. I instinctively wrap my arms around his neck and pull him closer to me. In response, he wraps his large arms around my back and pulled me into him as he continued to cry. Five minutes passed before his sobs start to lessen in frequency and intensity. All I could think about was the fact that my friend was devastated and he needed me.

    Eventually his cry was nothing more than muffled, very heavy breathing into my shoulder. He pulls away slightly and looks into my eyes; I don't recognize the look on his face. I have never seen him like this. I know my face is completely drenched with concern as I try to figure out what he is thinking. I don't have to ponder that thought for very long, because his lips press against mines.

His kisses start out slow and soft at first and then they increase in intensity. I don't know what is happening but every nerve ending in my body is awakened. I know I should stop him because he is not thinking clearly and very emotional; but I can't. His body feels too damn good pressed against mines. It's been so long since I have been held by a man. This is Antonio that we are talking about... *I have to stop him.* So I put my hand in the middle of his chest and push him away.

He looks at me with a hunger in his expression that I can't explain; and eyes that are wild with passion. He looks deep into my eyes and says only one word... "Please"...

after a brief moment passes, he kisses me again. He pounces on me and his mountainous frame knocks me back onto the couch, kissing me with ferocious intensity. This time I don't have the restraint to stop him. I allow myself to fall into his arms as I kiss him back. With every kiss my yearning for him grows and I grab a hand full of his hair, pulling his mouth deeper into mines.

He glides his hand along my calf and across my knee, finally coming to rest on my thigh. He hesitates momentarily, afraid I may stop him. When he receives no such objection from me, he gently massages my thigh and slowly continues to caress my leg until he locates my ass; he grabs a hand full of and lets out a low groan. I begin to feel vulnerable, because it was not until this moment that I became aware that I had on nothing but a towel. I usually don't do this with the lights on, but my mind is consumed with his sweet cologne and my body is so electrified with pleasure; that I don't even care.

When Love Isn't Enough

He continues to kiss me deeply as his hunger for me grows. He moves his other hand onto my thigh and grabs it so roughly that normally it would hurt but right now it brought me immense pleasure. I know he is ready for me as he pulls off my towel and lay on top of me. I become painfully aware that the only thing between me and intense pleasure is the thin layer of his clothing.

My hand starts to creep up the bottom of his shirt. Even without seeing his muscles I could feel their perfection. As he moved up and down grinding against my body I could feel the muscles in his back tense and relax. This turned me on more than I even knew possible, causing me to let out a low moan. He uses my expression of pleasure as his cue to continue. He was driving me absolutely crazy. Slowly, he moves his kisses from my mouth while he pulls my hair; forcing my head back and exposing my neck. He starts to kiss my neck with one hand still pulling my hair and the other creeping up my body towards my breast. This makes me slightly uncomfortable because I am self-conscious about my stomach; I stop him from moving his arm. He looks deep into my eyes, as if telling me to trust him; and he continues, seemingly unfazed by my momentary discomfort. He massages my breast gently which causes my nipple to become erect and my back to arch.

    He gazes into my eyes for a moment looking for the cause of my involuntary response. When he realizes t it was not a move of protest, or discomfort, he continues. He lifts my breast with his hand and moves his mouth from my neck down to my nipple, leaving a trail of kisses. He begins sucking my nipple very lightly as he makes figure 8's followed by nibbles using the tiniest amount of pressure. I have never felt such pleasure in my life. He gently clamps my nipple between his teeth and proceeds to turn his tongue into a vibrator and he moves my nipple quickly up and down with his tongue. I let out a soft moan as he let go of my hair and slowly moves that hand to my behind and grabs it pulling me closer into him.

He moves his mouth from my nipple to my ear and whispers, "I want you. Please let me have you Alayna". My body betrayed me at his request as it lets out a small shiver. I nodded and my eyes rolled into the back of my head feeling his warm breath on my ear. He pulls off his shirt and kisses me again. He slips a finger inside of my soft spot and begins to move it slowly at first and then the intensity increased.

My hands automatically roam to his boxers. He stands for just a moment staring longingly into my eyes, and pulls down his pants exposing himself. I stared at him pleased with what I am seeing as he reaches for his wallet and realizes he doesn't have a condom. He looks at me with an almost pleading glare and I realize that in that moment I did not care; my body was on fire.

He looks at me for confirmation and there was no rebuttal in my eyes. I reach out for him to come back to me. He lay on top of me and asked "are you sure?" "I have never been more sure of anything in my life" I say as I grab all of his manliness and placed it at my entry. He kissed me... and then he penetrates me... instant pleasure.

"My Heart Finally Said Enough Is Enough"

-My Dear Valentine

Chapter 11

I'm Tired

Victoria

I wake up the next morning still clinging to the slightest hangover from the night before. Squinting my eyes at the sunlight piercing through the window I reach my hand over to the night stand to turn off my alarm. I stretch and notice that Tahj is no longer in the bed. I get up, slip on my robe and make my way to the bathroom. I know the cure to my hangover is going to be dimming lights and taking a nice hot shower. I turn the dial on the bathroom lights until there was barely a glow emitting from the pot lighting in the ceiling and turn on the water in the rainfall shower so that it was just a little too warm and step inside.

The extra heat in the water feels great as it gently sears my skin. I decide although the extra hot water felt great on my body it probably wouldn't feel great on my head. I turn the heat down just a little and stick my head underneath the water and just sit there. After what felt like ten minutes, I decide to finally move on with my shower. I slowly wash my hair and then the rest of my body.

I step out of the shower and catch a glimpse of myself in the foggy mirror. I am beautiful but I still look overly tired due to the huge bags under my eyes. I need makeup and coffee to make it through the day. I hurriedly get dressed, picking out one of my scantiest swimsuits. I decide since I am in paradise I might as well dress the part. However, the wife in me kicked in and I decide to cover the swimsuit with a see through black cover up and shorts.

Tahj had set up this excursion so I was trying to dress the part. We were going to the rainforest today that had beautiful fresh water lagoons for swimming, but there would also be hiking... Lots of hiking... *she's trying to kill me...* I think amused with my reaction. I decide that tennis shoes would be the best thing to put on my feet. I slip into my black running shoes and threw my sandals into the bag.

I put my hair into a ponytail, fluff out my curls; put a light powder on my face. This was mostly to cover the dark circles under my eyes (because let's face it – it's going to be too damn hot to be walking around in a rainforest with a face full of thick makeup). I conclude that I will feel naked without my eyeliner and a little eyeshadow. After I make up my eyes, I put on one of the coral color lipsticks I brought that closely matched the color of my swimsuit. Now looking overly made up, I sigh and grab my backpack putting in just the necessities from my purse and lock it in the safe.

I take one last look in my room to make sure I didn't leave anything and step into the living area. I look around the room and it was relatively untouched, minus the

When Love Isn't Enough

coffee pot that sat full on the counter. I love Tahj, she read my mind. I walk over, find a coffee mug in one of the cabinets and pour myself a cup. I don't have to search for the sugar and creamer because Tahj had left that out for me. I put a little too much sugar and creamer into the cup (but let's face it, I like a little coffee with my cream and sugar) and take a sip... Perfection! I smile, and then set out in search for Tahj.

    I take a sip of my coffee and continue to scan the room. I notice a small opening in the French doors leading out to the balcony. I walk over to the balcony and open the door. I see Tahj sitting there with her IPad in one hand and her cell phone in the other, checking emails and drinking her coffee. My goodness I envy her! How does she just get up and get the day started like that without a moment's hesitation? She promised me that she wouldn't do any work while we were on the excursions or at the bar; but I should have known that she would not be able to pull herself away from her work completely.

Ensuring that she makes good on her promise, I decide to let her work in peace before we go on our excursion. I step out onto the balcony and sat in one of the oversized green chairs. I inhale deeply taking in the salty air as I look out into the sun. Tahj glances over in my direction letting me know that she acknowledged my presence, and then goes right back into her work. This observation makes me smile; her work ethic is impeccable.

I take another sip my coffee, grab a bagel that Tahj ordered from room service and fill it with some spread. I look out into the water and it's the most beautiful blue that you will ever see. I cannot believe that I am in paradise right now. Especially since three days ago, I didn't even know that we were going to be taking a trip. It really is nice having friends that can make things happen.

I gaze back into the water and feel the breeze once again on my face. *Gosh*, I think to myself, I could really do this every day of my life. I continue to eat my breakfast and lose myself in the water, occasionally sneaking a glance over at Tahj who was still diligently working. She was seemingly unfazed by the beauty surrounding us. As I get lost in my surroundings once more, I am left with thoughts about my life... and my unhappiness.

After saying my thoughts out loud to someone for the first time last night I felt like there was more to my story and I wasn't being honest with myself. What was I not telling myself? Not allowing myself to feel? What little detail was I missing? It can't just be that I am unhappy... What is the problem? What is my problem! My gaze continues to stretch the length of the horizon and then back to the other side. My mind wanders for what feels like thirty minutes, but in reality it was probably about five minutes. It is amazing the clarity that you get when you're in a place like this; I know almost instantaneously what has been eluding me for years.

When Love Isn't Enough

My problem is I have outgrown my husband. My problem is I want things in life that he doesn't want, and is unwilling to compromise. My problem is that he has allowed me to become complacent. When we were dating, he was always pushing me to be better and pushing me to go for that next promotion. He gave me courage, strength and stability necessary to conquer the impossible; that has all stopped now. My problem is we barely talk anymore and when we do talk it's either about the kids, work or our day, nothing substantive.

My problem is when I have tried to have this conversation with my husband in the past, I feel like he just tunes me out. I have told him that I was unhappy and what needed to change in our relationship for me to be happy. He just didn't listen! For example, my last two birthdays he didn't get me anything, not even a card. He did take me to a nice dinner but that wasn't even special. He had me make my own reservations and then paid for it with our joint bank account – so it was almost as if I paid for my own dinner. Don't get me wrong, I am not completely ungrateful for what he did, however, there was no thought put into it and it lacked originality.

Even last Christmas I had to ask him if we were exchanging gifts. Since we had children six years ago it has been all about them, and we hadn't exchanged a single gift. His response was, "I mean if you want me to get you something I will... I guess so". To this I replied, "Ok... I want you to", he asked me what I wanted and I told him something nice and to surprise me (I wanted him to have to put some thought into it). I spent the next two months picking out the perfect Christmas gift for him.

I had a watch engraved with his name on the back, but also on the face of the watch right under the makers' name. I knew that he liked Tungsten metal so I had it incorporated into the band. I also knew that he liked chocolate diamonds and I had one placed on each hour hand. I essentially designed his watch from scratch. I was so excited to give it to him! When Christmas day came I watched in anticipation as he opened his gift. He loved it and was giddy like a child. He put the watch on and gave me a big hug.

I was so excited to open my present that I couldn't stand it. It was a huge box so my imagination went wild. When I opened the wrapping paper my heart sunk but I tried not to let my face show my disappointment. As I stared at my gift, he said, "you know the vacuum cleaner has been on the fritz lately and I got tired of taking it into the shop."

Merry Christmas! ... That's right... after all I went through to pick out the perfect gift for him, this asshole got me a vacuum cleaner! Don't get me wrong, it's not the dollar amount that bothered me or even that he got me a vacuum cleaner because we did need one. What bothered me was the fact that this was my only gift and there was no real thought put into it.

When Love Isn't Enough

I know you sometimes get people gifts that will make their lives easier but that by no means should have been the only Christmas gift I received after a six year hiatus! We are not poor for Christ sake, we earn a good living, and he could have given me a proper gift. The worst part is the way he stood there and looked proud of himself, with his chest stuck out like a damn super hero that just saved the world! You could practically envision his cape blowing in the damn wind with his chest stuck out, and fists planted firmly on his sides. My daughters and I sat there looking dumbfounded.

My eldest daughter leaned over and whispered to me, "I wanted to get you some pretty earrings mommy because I know you like pearls. Daddy said, no no no honey, I think she will like this vacuum cleaner, look it even sucks up dog hair!" *Dog hair!!!* I thought to myself, *we don't even have a damn dog!* I wrinkled my face a little and thanked my baby girl for the kind gesture and thought to myself that our six year old knows more about proper gift giving than a grown ass man!

I wanted to rip that damn watch off his wrist and take it back to the store and get him a damn lawn mower, since ours is "on the brink of going out". My mature side kicked in, so I smiled and asked my babies to keep opening their gifts. The day moved on, blending into any other day, as I once again tried to wash the disappointment from my heart.

Then, there was Valentine's Day - which I never really cared about celebrating until I started to feel forgotten. I asked him yet again if we were exchanging gifts. He said his typical "sure if you want me to". Well I wanted him to. I mean you can't mess up Valentine's Day right? It's the holiday of love and there are gift ideas practically bursting out of the seams! You could literally walk into any Walgreens and find teddy bears and trinkets! He knows I love teddy bears and I decided that I would be happy to receive one if that was what he got me. I just knew he would nail this one. Well once again I was wrong.

The problem started when I began a diet the month before Valentine's Day and I had been arguing with my husband about bringing unhealthy food in the house. I didn't feel like he was supporting me by encouraging unhealthy behavior. His response to my concern was that I should have the will power to just not eat it. After several fights about it he said that he would try harder to support my weight loss goal. After a few weeks of gift hunting for my husband, I had come up with the perfect gift once again. What did he get me? A box of chocolates! That's right, *chocolate* while he knows I am on a diet. He could have gotten me *ANYTHING* else at that point! That was the icing on the freaking cake!

I should be grateful that I am getting anything at all right? There are people that don't get anything (hell I was one of them for a while there). Gifts can't be good and thoughtful all of the time right? I think back to the beginning of our relationship, prior to marriage and kids and we never really did anything major on the holidays. The major difference was, back then, throughout the year, he made me feel like every day was a holiday.

It was the little things like a card just saying I love you or a single rose in various colors with a little poem saying what the color meant. It was the random date nights and flowers he sent to my job. He gave me massages whenever I wanted them and I really felt like a queen. He would buy me jewelry just because he saw it and made him think of me. These acts of kindness and love made it ok that we ignored the big stuff. He is now ignoring the little stuff too, so the big stuff seems more significant.

Valentine's Day was the final straw for me. I told my husband that I was unhappy and that I was starting to question the status of our marriage. I told him all of my concerns and that I felt unappreciated and ignored. He did absolutely nothing to change any of it. I think that's what hurt the most, you know what I mean? That I actually took the time to describe in detail how I felt and what needed to change and he took no action. How much is a girl supposed to put up with? I feel like my husband doesn't understand that I have needs and feelings, because I am always so strong. I am always the rock of our family, holding everyone and everything down; but a girl gets tired.

I also reflect on the fact that over the years, he has "talked" to several different girls. He never slept with them or kissed them and that was always his argument; but he did it behind my back and I found out about it. His argument was that he wasn't doing what my exes did to me because they actually cheated on me. Every time he would say it, his words stung like a scorpion to my soul. Why does he have to bring them up? Why does he have to make such a low blow? I know he was trying to make a point for himself but didn't he realize that in doing so he brought us something deeply personal for me. The fact that I had dealt with so much infidelity made me insecure and it made me feel like I wasn't good enough?

I would instantly shut down because he made me feel guilty, and like I should be appreciative that he wasn't "completely" cheating on me. He wanted me to feel that somehow what he was doing was better. He would tell me to stop nagging him about it and he would stop talking to the girl if it made me happy. I don't understand, shouldn't it make you happy not to do it? Shouldn't you stop doing something you know is hurting me, simply because it is hurting me?

Obviously, he didn't understand that concept either because six months later, we were having the same conversation about a different girl. The worst part was finding out about it every time. I know the old saying *you shouldn't go looking for things if you don't want to find it.* That was some bullshit created by men who were tired of getting caught cheating and women that were too damn fragile to handle the truth! There shouldn't be anything for me to find when I look... that is the whole damn point. If you can go through my shit and not find anything, why should I be subjected to finding shit on yours?

I am sure he was just measuring the size of his dick! Looking to see if he *"still had it"* and that was what all of these different women were about. He did it even though he knew it hurt me and that it bothered me... he still did it. I spent our entire marriage with my attention solely on him. I didn't text guys, call guys, or flirt with guys. I didn't as much as glance in another guy's direction out of respect for my husband and our relationship. Not even a glance! It wasn't for the lack of guys trying; I had guys trying to get my attention all of the time. I just simply ignored them. If my husband only knew the number of guys that tried to get my attention it would make him insecure. I only had eyes for him for ten years and too much respect for him to hurt him.

When Love Isn't Enough

He took that for granted… He took me for granted… and I would tell him that, all the time. I always insisted that he would not like it if I did to him what he was doing to me. He always insisted that he would not care. I told him that I hope he never had to find out how it felt; because that would be the day I stop caring about his feelings. That would be the day he would find out how I have felt all of those years; the day he has to find out how it feels to have to compete with another man for my attention.

Well, that day is here because **I am tired** … I am sick and tired of being tired. **I am tired** of constantly doing the right thing; **I am tired** of playing mom all of the time and never putting any time and energy into myself; **I am tired** of never getting to have any fun because I am too busy worrying about making sure everyone else is having fun; **I am tired** of being completely taken for granted by everyone in my life. **I am tired** of just being expected to be normal all of the time. **I am tired** of having to be "emotion free" for the sake of everyone else's damn comfort level. **I am tired** of having to hold myself together and my emotions together not only at home, but: at work, at the PTA meetings, with my family, with my children and with my friends. **I. Am. Tired.** Even after my pregnancy losses... *I WAS THE ONE CONSOLING EVERYBODY; I WAS THE STRONG ONE.* I was more worried about their wellbeing than my own. People tried to comfort me but I was so worried about their emotional state that I never really allowed myself to openly grieve for fear of upsetting them. **I AM TIRED...** *OF DOING THE RIGHT THING... ALL... OF... THE... TIME!!!* **I am tired. I am tired of being tired.**

"You see what you want to see. The mask shows a part of me. Look Deeper inside and see the real me"

-Dr. Laverne Jackson-Harvey

The Mask

Chapter 12
The Mask

Tahj

I had just finished the final sentence to the last email I was going to send today. I sigh to myself and think how good it feels to be done. I mean I love my job but it's a little frustrating that I am in paradise working. I bent my neck from side to side letting out a small crack. Sometimes my job can be so stressful; but I love it... It's my baby. I know I promised Victoria that I wouldn't do work while we were on the excursions, at the bar or the beach, but I never promised her I wouldn't do any work at all.

If I ignore my work for a couple of days I would come back to a complete shit storm. My office would literally fall apart without me for too long. Note to self, I need to develop some more leaders that can take on some of my responsibilities. Luckily, I have Tom and he is very good at his job. He can respond to non-critical needs but he always left the more complicated things for me. It was amazing having a reliable assistant. I don't know what I would do without him.

    I glance at Victoria and she is just sitting there patiently waiting and letting me work. She is not letting the fact that I am working bother her so that I can focus on what I need to. This is why I love her and she is my best friend, she understands me in a way that no one else does. I look out over the water and acknowledge for the first time all morning how beautiful it is. It's the most perfect shade and mixture of Purex and Aqua blues. I close my eyes and my other senses awaken and take in everything around me. I feel the soft breeze that dances across my face and arms. The same breeze brushes ever so gently across my hair. The air is so warm and thick with moisture that you can almost taste the salt. I hear birds in the distance getting closer and waves rushing over the shore. This rhythmic sound continues in the background of my thoughts one wave after the other. Tom has really outdone himself with these reservations.

I open my eyes and see the birds from my meditation, flying by and think that this really is paradise. I am reminded of my conversation with Victoria last night and I am troubled by it. I hate to see my friend hurting and hearing that she and Max were having trouble, but I can't say that I am surprised. I think I always knew this day would come but did not speak my opinions because I feared being labeled as a "hater", so I just kept my thoughts to myself. If she liked it I loved it, not to mention that I was in no position to give advice, having been married and divorced by twenty-four.

Victoria had always been one of those people that was full of fire, full of life. She was the life of the party and had one of those infectious personalities that could win over even the grumpiest of people. She always had a very "robust" dating life to put it tastefully.... Oh hell, the truth is she changed men like she changed underwear. Hell, sometimes she even wore two or three pairs of underwear at the same time.

I glance nervously at Victoria afraid that she might hear my thoughts. If she knew what I was thinking she might try to kill me. I chuckle, Victoria is so deep in thought that she doesn't even notice. She appears to be in a trance as she stares out over the water. My thoughts continue to flood over me like the waves of the ocean.

I remember the day that she met Max at that Kappa party. Max came along and he changed her. Not in a bad way, it's like he grew her up in a sense. He was very different than any guy she had ever dated. He was very mature, kind and thoughtful. Victoria always had a bad boy complex from the time that we were small. She always loved guys that kept things exciting and new, but they often hurt her, and left her broken. Max was safe and she needed him and he needed her. He needed her to break him out of his shell and make him comfortable within himself. They were a perfect match and everyone could see it.

That is everyone except for me. I didn't say it at the time because I was just happy to see my friend happy and being treated the way she deserved to be treated. However, I always wondered if he would be too plain for her. I wondered if she would miss the fire inside of her that was never completely extinguished, but continued to smolder inside of her quietly underneath the surface in darkness. I wondered if she would outgrow him and get bored. They had been together for so long and built a wonderful life together so I thought, maybe I was wrong.

That is until last night when she confirmed my worst fear for her. I know there is more to the story but I do not think now is the time to pry since we are on our way to having a day of fun. At some point, we will have the conversation because I saw a lot of sadness and pain underneath her mask of happiness. She had perfected that mask. My thoughts are interrupted by an alarm I set on my phone telling me that it is time to go (You know I love my alarms). I laugh loudly at my last thought and the fact that I catch Victoria jump in my peripheral, at the sound of my alarm. She must have been in extremely deep thought. She looks at me and rolls her eyes, causing another chuckle to escape me.

    Victoria gets up and grabs her coffee mug and plate and walks back into the room. I take one last glimpse of the water and grab my stuff and follow her inside. I already have on my swimsuit and shorts; I just need to grab my cover up and my bag. I head over to the sink and place my dishes there, go into my bedroom to get the things I need. This should be fun... I roll my eyes and sigh.

    I really don't know what Tom was thinking setting *me* up with an outdoor hiking excursion. I think that was his idea of a joke; he must have lost his mind. I told myself that I would try new things and be open to new experiences, so that is fully what I intend to do. After I slip on my tennis shoes taking a cue from Victoria I grab my off (we don't need Zika problems) and lock my possessions in the safe.

    Back in the living area Victoria is already waiting and Facetiming with her kids. I take the prompt from another alarm and I let her know that it is time to go. She says good bye to her children and we step out of our room and into the warm sun, ready to partake in our adventure. I remember Tom saying that we needed to bring rain gear. I run back into the room and grab the two ponchos that he gave me, shove them and a few cold waters into my bag and step back out into the sun.

When Love Isn't Enough

Sometimes you meet somebody and you know in that moment that they are going to change your life so completely, forever.

-Ella York

Chapter 13

El Yunque

We make our way down past the lobby to the area where the shuttles pick up hotel patrons and take them to their various excursions. I feel the beads of sweat already beginning to form on my forehead. *This is such a bad idea,* I think to myself. I literally hate the heat and don't think I could ever live anywhere more humid than Charlotte. I can barely stand the extreme heat that we have there, and it only lasts for about a month.

If I hadn't divorced my husband and needed a change of scenery I would never have followed Victoria anywhere warm. I was desperate and needed a change of scenery to start over, so I applied, got a pretty good job for an entry level position and the rest is history.

It's actually pretty amazing how we all ended up in in Minnesota and then in Charlotte. Victoria and I were originally from Milwaukee, WI and went to college in Minnesota because of reciprocity. Alayna was from St. Cloud, MN and went to the University of Minnesota (U of M) because she received a scholarship. Aria literally picked schools out of a book and happened to get in. Desi went to the U of M because she wanted to get as far away from her family in Texas as she could. Her other options were too expensive so she ended up in Minnesota.

Desi is actually the one that brought us to Charlotte, NC in the first place. After doing internships at her company while in college, upon graduation they offered her a position, but she had to move to Charlotte. Victoria was having a hard time getting a good job and Desi was able to get her a position. They moved after Victoria convinced her husband to move and he was able to get a job. After Victoria left, Alayna was by herself in MN (because I had moved

When Love Isn't Enough

back to Milwaukee to be with my husband) and decided that she wanted to be with her sisters. She wasn't having much luck finding a good job anyway, so she got into a temp agency, packed her car and came down. No matter how we ended up in NC, I was grateful to have us all together again after my divorce. These ladies were my backbone and helped to keep me sane (even though Desi drove me crazy sometimes).

 My thoughts are interrupted by Victoria getting to her feet when they call the name for our excursion "El Yunque". "El Yunque – is a rainforest located in Puerto Rico and is the only Tropical Rainforest that belongs to the US Forest Service", I hear the driver say as we made our way up several windy paths to get to our destination. As we reach the entrance to the rainforest I feel my mouth drop. There are towering mountains covered in trees. It reminds me a lot of the Asheville, NC Mountains back home. There is one subtle difference; there is a cloudy mist that looms over the mountains surfaces.

Almost as if he were reading my mind, the driver tells us that "the mountain of Pico El Yunque stands at 1080 meters above sea level and it is almost always covered in a thin mist due to its high humidity. This humidity sometimes prompts downpours that are isolated through various parts of the Rainforest, but almost impossible for a meteorologist to identify". I grab my bag a little closer suddenly appreciative for Tom buying me those ponchos, and Victoria for prompting me to wear tennis shoes.

We sit in an area with all of the other tourists and are given instructions about the rules and different emergency procedures while on the mountain and hiking trails. We are told that we would visit several fresh water sites that are located within El Yunque and then split into groups with various tour guides based on our hiking skill level and preference to visit the fresh water sources. We obviously picked the group that did an easy hiking trail and spent more time in the water. Once everyone is separated into their groups we begin our hike.

It is challenging at first and the slight burn that I feel in my legs feels nice, leaving my muscles yearning for more. I didn't realize it had been three days since I worked out (that is a long time for me). I look over at Victoria and realize I am fairing a little better than she is at the moment and let out a laugh.

As we made our way through the dense trees on a thin trail that was placed perfectly in the middle, I started to become hyper aware of my surroundings. There are mountainous trees as far as the eye can see, many of which are linked together by vines. I see so many flowers and plants that have extremely bright colors and hear various animal noises in the distance. Many of them sound like chirps or squawks and there is something that sounds like cicadas. I begin to warm up to the beauty of this place.

When Love Isn't Enough

Something catches my eye that is most disturbing because it doesn't belong there. It literally stops me in my tracks. I take a second glance to see if I am dreaming, but I am not; it is there as clear as day. Hanging off one of the vines is a black rose (with a hint of purple), perfect and open, glistening with the tiniest amount of dew. This revelation causes me to stumble and Victoria catches my arm. I try to find the words to describe to Victoria what I am seeing but there is no need. She is staring at it as well, just as shocked as I am at its presence.

We reflexively reach for our jewelry; me for bracelet and Victoria, her ring. In that moment as humid as it is in this rainforest, I feel an icy chill run down my spine. My thoughts are jerked immediately to Arya and it almost brings me to my knees. I haven't seen a black rose since the day we buried her besides the one I wear on my bracelet in her memory.

When Love Isn't Enough

The day that Arya died was one of the worst days of my life. She is the reason we are all friends now. She brought us together in life and kept us bonded in death. I always like getting together with the girls because it feels like Arya is there with us somehow. After she died and we identified her body a few days later, we went to set up a memorial at the crash site. When we got there we saw four black roses growing out of the concrete amongst the debris. It was the strangest thing because roses don't grow out of concrete; and definitely not in the middle of winter in Minnesota! We picked the roses and each took one.

When we had her funeral service after her parents arrived a week later, we were once again greeted with black roses growing near her gravesite. We looked at each other as if we had seen a ghost. Her mother came over to us, having seen us staring at the roses and told us the story of why Arya had a black rose tattoo on her wrist. She told us that Arya thought that the black rose symbolized something different than most people. She thought it symbolized eternal life.

After the loss of her grandmother, she got the tattoo against the approval of other people in her community in India. She told her mother, to her, it symbolized life after death and was a dark flame burning through time and space continuously reborn. I must have looked confused because she continued. You see... Every other rose when it wilts it changes color and loses its magnificence. When a black rose dies it is still black, never losing anything from its glory. It is the one rose that does not lose value in death. Therefore, it is eternally alive.

I am interrupted by one of the tour guides tapping me on the shoulder with a concerned look on his face. "Estas bien?" I look confused. "I'm sorry I don't speak Spanish". "Oh sorry, are you okay?" His accent is so thick and rich it finally brought me out of my trance enough to take in his appearance. He had a military build and jet black hair that lay perfectly to the side; his skin was caramel perfection. His smile reveals a perfect set of bright white teeth.

    This man was absolutely breathtaking and right now he was showing a look of extreme concern as frown lines crease his brow. "I'm fine" I responded clumsily. "I must have overheated and just need to get some water". He seems satisfied with this response and hands me a cold bottle of water. I catch Victoria's worried glance and knew that she was not buying my story but she also looks as though she understands what is bothering me.

    The tour guide gives me a parting glance and walks back up to the front of the group. I caught the look of a few straggling tourists but eventually everyone continued forward. Victoria asked me if I was okay; I nodded, she grabs my arm and we continue down the trail. I become lost in the nature surrounding me once more. I hear the tour guide announce up ahead that we are nearing our first fresh water destination. He tells us that if we want to swim in this fresh water lagoon we could.

Thank goodness because I was starting to get hot as hell on this hike and the idea of getting into a fresh water pool sounds very good. We arrive at the pier and inside the water was so blue and crystal clear, you could literally see down to the bottom. There were large plants and vines that made up the walls of the lagoon. Sprinkled amongst the plants were colorful flowers and I even saw a few parrots flying by overhead. He tells us how this was one of many self-purified fresh water sources in El Yunque and that we will have the opportunity to visit some of the others later in the day.

They warned us that the large rocks inside the water were very slippery, and that we should be careful getting in and out. I look over at Victoria, and laugh; she must have been hot also because she was already half way stripped and taking off her necklace. She read my mind; we look at each other and let out a small giggle at our high level of enthusiasm.

We stepped to the edge of the stairs, counted to three and jump in. *HOLY SHIT*! This water is the absolute coldest thing that I have ever been submersed in. I let out a scream and the tour guides laugh at us. It was cold as hell! How could they not warn us? I became angered by the thought that they did it on purpose and decide to let them have it!

"How dare you not tell me how cold it is before I jumped in there? This thing needs to come with a God damn warning sign! I am freezing and then your ass is over there laughing like something is funny". Victoria shot me a warning glance, but I do not care and continue, "It is your job to make sure that I am making a well informed decision and I have all of the information necessary about any particular thing in this Rainforest that may impact me. *This water is cold as hell* asshole!

All three of them look shocked at first, but then the one that helped me earlier smirks and his look of shock turns into amusement. "Well ma'am, I do my best to make sure that all of my patrons are well informed and hydrated at all times (he winked at me). I made sure you had all of the necessary information; but if you had asked about the temperature of the water I would have told you it was roughly forty degrees Fahrenheit all year round."

He was really enjoying himself now, his smirk turned into a full on grin. "So now that you are inquiring ma'am; do be careful entering the water, as it is 40 degrees and very cold. I also hear that it is 'cold as hell' according to some patrons (he shot a crooked smile at me once more); although I am a little confused by this because, although I have not been there personally, I have been told that hell is a pretty warm place".

I couldn't help but smile at his sarcastic ass response. Victoria stood on the

When Love Isn't Enough

rock next to me laughing hysterically, *Traitor*. He reaches out a hand to me and asks if I need help getting out of the water. At that moment I look into his eyes and realize how beautiful they are. I couldn't explain what I felt as I stare into his eyes, but we had an undeniable connection. I had to resist the urge to grab his hand and pull him into the water. I dart my eyes away as he sat there with his hand extended. Even though I am cold, I felt warm inside when I thought about him; however, there is no way my pride will let him help me out of this water. So I say, "No thank you" and swim away. Victoria smirks at him one more time and swam behind me.

"My goodness he is handsome", she says when we were out of ear shot. I smirk and giggle; she continues, "And he knows how to put you in your place... I like him already". In response to her comment I splash her with water, we laugh and begin chasing each other across the lagoon like school girls. We really are having a great time and the more time we spend in the water the more it feels like it is room temperature. I must admit that I am a little disappointed when the tour guide announces it is time to go to the next phase of our trip.

I cannot get the connection I have with him out of my mind, but I will not entertain it. I am not looking for anything serious here on this island. We climb out of the lagoon slowly, being careful not to slip. I reach the top stair and I turn around and look at this beautiful place one last time. I will have to take a picture before I leave.

I turn to walk back to my clothes and I catch our handsome, smart mouthed tour guide staring at me. I walk over to Victoria and grab my towel. Out of my peripheral vision I notice that he is still staring, and being more obvious than before. It was almost as if he is trying to get my attention, but I will not oblige him.

I dry myself with a towel from head to toe, and in that moment, I am grateful that I had done that extra cardio before we left. I put back on my shorts and cover up, throw on my large shades and continue to pretend that I didn't see him. He was becoming more difficult to ignore as I catch a glimpse of him scanning my whole body with his eyes, making frequent stops on my behind. So of course I turn it a little bit so that he can get a better look. Victoria observes this exchange, smirks, and walks away. Where the hell is she going?

Out of the corner of my eye I see the handsome tour guide walking over to me. So that's why she left, *traitor*! I need to get some new friends! He reaches out his hand "Diego, pleasure to meet you" he says in his sexy accent. "Tahj and the pleasure is mine" I blush, "So I guess we better get going, we have a long hike ahead of us" I say as I walk away from him not looking back.

We stop halfway through for lunch, and Diego was still staring at me; but not in a strange way, in a nervous way. We finish our lunch and make our way to a different pier where we will be completing the second part of our excursion, a boat ride around parts of the island. Our old tour guides leave us with a set of new guides.

I look at the crew that will be manning our boat and my eyes stop at the bartender. I shoot a glance at Victoria whose face says that she is thinking the same. How did Diego get onto the boat without us seeing him? The bartender then locks eyes with me and I glance over nervously at Victoria as he walks over to us. I look up at him and notice subtle differences; I know that he is not Diego. This man had the same caramel kissed complexion, but he was more slender in build and slightly taller. However, he is still just as handsome, with those same gorgeous eyes.

He catches us staring at him with confused looks and offers us a drink. We are too stunned by the similarities and don't answer immediately. Finally, I get out the words "two white wines please" he smiles and walks away. Victoria leans into me and says "What the hell is up with all of these fine damn men?" We smirk as he walks back over to us "Here you are ladies".

He looks into our eyes once more and says "I don't mean to sound crazy but do I know you? You were looking at me as if we have met before". Victoria is the first to respond "Actually we were trying to figure out if you were on the first part of the tour with us".

Understanding washes over his face and he replies, "No, that was my brother Diego; people often say that we look like twins". He extends his hand to Victoria first and then to me, "My name is Alejandro, but you can call me Alex". "Hello Alex my name is Victoria and this is Tahj", she says with a nervous smile.... *Uh Oh!* I know that look. It has been a while since I have seen it but I know that look. *Victoria is a goner.*

"Anything that gets your blood racing is probably worth doing"

-Hunter S Thompson

Chapter 14
Lust at First Sight
Victoria

Oh my goodness, this man is absolutely gorgeous. I have never seen anyone that looked like him before – well that hadn't stepped out of a magazine anyway. He is breathtaking! His body is slender and perfectly chiseled; his eyes the perfect shade of brown. He walks with a confidence that let me know he knew he looked good.

I am in trouble and I knew it the moment he told me his name was Alex. Tahj just gave me that *girl be careful look*, and turns away. There was something about him that made my blood flow faster and my heart skip a beat. Be careful? I stare into his eyes which gazed back at me with a ferocious intensity; I immediately know that "careful" is not an option with him. At this thought a warm sensation shot through my body. What is happening here? Why is my body reacting this way? Staring at him my blood raced even faster, eventually turning into a full on sprint.

I don't know if it's because I have spent the last ten years not looking at another man and I have finally allowed myself to look, or if there was just no one that ever caught my body's attention the way he has? Whatever the reason, when I saw him, and he saw me... We connected in a way that I can't even begin to explain. I close my eyes and concentrate hard trying to regain control of my body and my mind. I need to keep our interactions friendly because my mind is still not made up about my husband.

He continues to bring us drinks whenever our glass needs a refill. While he serviced the other clients he keeps stealing glances at me. I try not to stare back but I just can't help it because he is so damn good looking. I bet women fawn over him all the time. As our eyes connect once again, it feels as if we are speaking without words. It's like our bodies are sending out a silent Morse code.

Every time my glass gets close to being empty he is right there with a refill and I begin to wonder if he is doing it on purpose. Maybe he is trying to get me drunk so he can take advantage of me. Living in my thoughts my heart crumbles. I have always thought of myself as an attractive woman but he makes me insecure. He makes me wonder if I am good enough – I instinctively wrap my left arm over my right and stare down at the ground. I don't like this feeling, but I think it's my minds way of protecting itself because there is just no way this man is into me. I am sure he can have any woman he wants.

We dock at the next stop on our excursion. I hadn't even noticed that the boat slowed down because I was so engulfed in my thoughts. I notice that people are already heading to the back of the boat and my bartender is already gone. Tahj and I take off our shoes, leave them by our seats (there is nothing worse than sandy shoes) and make our way to the back of the boat.

I look around and see my bartender... my Alex... helping people off of the boat. What is my problem? I am already claiming him for myself? This is ludicrous! As the line starts to get shorter and we get closer to where is he standing I catch a glimpse of him as his muscles flex underneath his fitted shirt. My heart skips a beat, I don't know what he is doing to me but I like it.

He reaches out a hand to me to help me off the boat. I grab it without thinking and I feel electricity where our skin makes contact. I don't look at him because I fear the flush of my cheeks will give me away. Why is my body betraying me this way? We make our way up the beach and for the first time since the boat docked Alex is not in my view. Without the distraction of Alex, I am finally allowed to take in the beauty of the beach.

When Love Isn't Enough

  White sand is painted across the shoreline as far as the eye can see. I step into the water and notice the warmth of the water. It's so much warmer than the water from the lagoon. I look down and I can see my feet in clear water that has a beautiful aqua tint. This place truly is paradise. I see Tahj moving ahead of me and I follow suit. We find the bar on the beach and grab a tequila sunrise. I take a sip and it's good; I feel the rum go down my throat warming it ever so slightly. We walk over to a set of beach chairs and lay out our towels, take off our shorts and cover ups. I rub on suntan lotion and look around the beach searching for Alex. He is nowhere to be found and I am really disheartened, secretly hoping that he has not left us for the day.

  I lie on my chair and put in my headphones. I am feeling tropical so I decide to play Diole's *Chikiti Bomba* and I let the warmth of the sun wash over me. The song transitions in the *Lean On Remix*, by Major Lazer and I open my eyes because I feel Tahj shift. Alex is standing over me. I jump up a little too quickly and he lets out a small chuckle; dammit, even his laugh is sexy. How the hell can a laugh be sexy? I am in so much trouble. He asks me if he could talk to me in private. I look a Tahj, she nods and smirks. He grabs my hand and helps me up. Again, I shudder at his touch and follow him over to a shaded area by the bar.

"So, tell me about yourself Amor." he says in his velvety voice. I started like I would with anyone else, "My name is Victoria, I have two kids, I work in marketing, and I am married…" *whoops! I can't believe I lead with that.* I knew for a fact that he would be done talking to me after I divulged that piece of information, but he didn't even flinch – I am not going to lie, I am disappointed. It confirmed what I knew all along, that he isn't interested in me. I continue to tell him about myself and where I am from.

Then, he tells me about himself; he is twenty-eight with no kids, and not really looking for anything too serious. He is just

When Love Isn't Enough

living his life one day at a time. *Great!* I think sarcastically, rolling my eyes. He continues as if not noticing my slip up, telling me that he was born and raised in Puerto Rico. I stare into his eyes listening to him speak and he stops mid-thought. His abrupt stop startles me and I stare at him confused. He pauses for a moment and then continues his tone different this time, conflicted, "There is just something about you that draws me to you, and I can't explain it. I want to be away from you and not look at you, but I can't pull away. It makes me feel like I am going crazy". My heart skips several beats at that moment and I can't do anything but look at him... "Igual" I respond; he smiles at my response.

"You speak Spanish Amor? Is this your first time in Puerto Rico? He asks. I respond "It is my first time, but it will surely not be my last. It's beautiful here, and I now have an incentive to come back." I blush and continue, "We weren't even supposed to come to Puerto Rico, but my friend decided at the last minute she wanted to come here."

He pauses and then speaks, "I am not sure what made your friend want to come here, but I am glad that you came. I feel like I am supposed to meet you. What a cruel twist of fate that you are married?" I looked down blushing. He moves on, once again without acknowledging my shame, "I want to show you the real Puerto Rico tonight. Let me and my brother take you and your friend out tonight. You can even meet us there if you don't want me to know where your hotel is. This tourist stuff is nothing; let me show you something real". I thought about it for 2.5 seconds; I almost think it was out of habit that I even paused, because I knew my answer immediately – before he even finished his question – yes.

    Tahj is just going to have to live with being voluntold for this little outing. She can thank me later when she is hanging out with his handsome brother. Alex responds "great, can I see your phone?" I give it to him and he put his number in my phone; "Is it ok to send a text from your phone to mines so I have your number?" I nod yes.

When Love Isn't Enough

He tells me to text him my hotel information and that he has to go back to work but is excited about seeing me later tonight. He grabs my hand, kisses it, and says, "it really is a pleasure to meet you".

I cannot hide my body's response to this. My smile is wider than my face and my cheeks turn bright red, *all I needed were big shoes and I could have been a clown.* He smiles at my response, "Bye Victoria" and walks away. At the sound of my name coming out of his mouth in his beautiful accent, I felt my body flood with pleasure and anticipation.

Tahj saw him leave and pulls down her shades to look at me over the top. I sigh and giggle; she makes me feel like I was doing the walk of shame the whole time I walk over to her. She says "You miss thing have some explaining to do Victoria Ann!!!" I laugh and tell her that the only thing I am explaining to her is we have a date tonight; she looks perplexed. I roll my eyes, sit down and tell her about my conversation with

Alex and how he made me feel. To this she responded "be careful, I want you to make sure you know what you are doing".

Saying all of this out loud made me sad and ashamed. Tahj did not show any sign of breaking, "I love you and support you wherever your journey leads you. My main concern is that you are happy". I sit and wallow in my sad reality until Tahj asks for more details about the date. I tell her I set her up with his fine brother, to which she high fives me. "Since we are going on a date we need to go shopping to find something to wear". I ponder this for a moment, but I am emotionally drained from the events and revelations of today, I need to collect my thoughts before tonight. I tell her I will meet her back at the room.

We took the boat back to the dock with a constant drink in hand. I sneak a glance at Alex whenever I have the opportunity, wondering about the promise of tonight and what it will bring. My nerves then sink in… What have I done?

When Love Isn't Enough

"Maybe I'm scared because you mean more to me than any other person. You are everything I think about, everything I need, everything I want"

-Hplyrikz

Chapter 15

The Morning After

Alayna

The next morning I awaken to Antonio in my bed and I think to myself, *what the hell did we do last night?* I grab my lips out of instinct and the memory of his kiss floods over causing me to bite my lip out of habit. His kisses were heavenly; I have never felt anything like it. All of these feelings of pleasure don't negate the fact that I have now slept with one of my best friends. That thought brings me back to reality and it causes my face to wrinkle as I let out a sigh.

I watch him sleep peacefully and I can't help but worry about what he will think when he wakes up? How will he feel? Is he going to regret what happened last night? As much as I am confused by last night, I would never be able to use a word like regret to describe what happened. Last night was magical. Last night was wonderful. Last night was amazing. Last night was everything I could never have thought to dream for. He was incredibly tender, caring and loving... I never knew making love could be like that. This is my friend and that complicates things, in a major way.

I can't believe we just did that, but then I feel how my body responds to memories of last night- tensing and relaxing- and I somehow know I want it to happen again. I get up and go to the bathroom, because I really don't want him to see me looking completely disheveled when he wakes up. I run water over my face; trying to wash away yesterday's memories... it does not work. I look at myself in the mirror wondering if my look reflects how I feel.

I am slightly disappointed because I thought that somehow feeling magical would change my appearance. I stare back at my reflection and I see that I still look just as plain as ever. Having amazing sex changed nothing. I don't know why I am so hard on myself. I know that I am a cute girl by normal guy standards. It's just that I didn't think that someone like him would find me desirable, he is physically perfect. This thought frightens me because it makes me feel that he can't possibly know what he did last night. It had to be a mistake, and that thought bothers me.

I shake my head in the mirror, grab my toothbrush and brush my teeth. The last thing he will get is morning breath from me. I use the bathroom, wash my hands, and run a brush through my hair, put on a neutral colored lipstick, and grab my cute nighties hanging on the back of the door. *It's not going to get any better than this* I think to myself. With one last parting glance I turn to leave the bathroom. I open the door and he is standing there looking at me with a delighted expression.

When Love Isn't Enough

"Good morning beautiful, how are you?" he says. I stare at him shocked at his chipper demeanor and all I can manage to get out is "fine". Inside I was screaming *I am excellent, I am wonderful! Last night was amazing, you were amazing* but I couldn't get my thoughts together enough to form the words, so "fine" will have to be enough. He walks over to me and moves the hair from my shoulder, exposing the nape of my neck. I turn my back to him. In response to this he kisses my newly exposed neck. In response to his kiss my body lets out a series of small involuntary shivers. He grabs me around my waist and turns me gently back around. "Why are you hiding from me sweetheart? What's wrong?" As he spoke he almost looked concerned.

I blurt out my words so fast that they were almost unintelligible "What do you mean what's wrong? You are one of my best friends and I don't know where we stand after last night. You don't feel strange around me? It's doesn't complicate your emotions to look at me? I don't know what to think. I don't want to lose you as my friend. I didn't want it to be like this. We have been friends for so long that I don't want to mess this up". In response to my rant he smiles. I am not going to lie that pissed me off.

He pauses for a little too long, causing me to shift uncomfortably; and then he continues, "Listen, you were, and still are one of my best friends. You helped me last night when I needed you the most and I am eternally grateful for that". *Grateful*! Did he just say grateful? *Oh hell no*! You do not have sex with a girl and then say that you are 'grateful'! Who the hell does that? I am pissed and now my face has turned into a frown.

He acted as though he didn't see my reaction, "It wasn't my intention to be with you that way when I came over here last night. I just knew that I was heartbroken and I needed you. When I looked into your eyes it was like our souls bonded in a way that they never had before, and I didn't want to be apart from you any longer. I saw something in your eyes that I hadn't seen before; maybe it was because I was so wrapped up in my own life and in my own relationship, but I liked what I saw! You are one of the best people that I have ever met in this world with one of the most beautiful souls. I am grateful for you and I always will be."

There goes that damn word again. He's grateful. He had better not use that word again or I might just punch him in the throat. More than I was offended by his being "grateful" (like I provided some sort of charity service), I am hurt that sex with me was not what he wanted. It sounded more like an involuntary choice that he made as he looked into my eyes and "saw something". I immediately feel like the rebound and it devastates me.

I look up and he is looking at me with a concerned expression. He continues very carefully, "I don't know what to say about last night and I don't know if it means anything more; but what I will say is that I love you enough as my friend and as a person to try. I love you enough to explore these feelings and see where they lead us; and I love you enough that no matter what the outcome is I will do my best to make sense of this mess. I promise you that one way or another I will make this right for you, even if I have to spend the rest of my life trying. I want you to always be in my life in some capacity. You mean the world to me. And I thank you".

By the end of his response I was a very disheartened. I don't know what I thought was going to happen; but I didn't expect to feel like the rebound as much as I do. I was slightly deflated hearing that last night wasn't as passionate and wonderful for him as it was for me; That everything for him was based off of a look, a momentary lapse of judgment. Hearing his thoughts does not feel good and it makes me sad. I feel the emotion wash over my face at a rate that I could not control.

When Love Isn't Enough

I can no longer maintain my composure, and silent tears start to roll down my face.

He lifts my face and stares into my eyes as if trying to communicate something to me. All I can muster is a small, indignant "What?" as I pull my face away and look back down at the ground; too ashamed to look into his eyes. He lifts my face once more, and this time he spoke, "I am going to have a hard time being your friend because now that I know what it's like to feel your lips, be wrapped in your arms and have me inside of you, I don't think I can stay away from you. In fact, I don't think that I can be without you. I look into your eyes and I want to feel you again. I want to make love to you and I am very conflicted about this."

"Why are you telling me this" I asked in a quiet, almost mouse like voice. "I can see on your face that you are concerned I didn't enjoy being with you and it would be a gross injustice for you to not know what you do to me physically." I don't know if he was trying not to hurt my feelings or if he truly felt that way. I didn't have a lot of time to process his words, because his lips came crashing into mines with a fiery passion.

We watched the sunrise from the floor as we made love.

"The biggest adventure you can take is to live the life of your dreams."

-Oprah Winfrey

Chapter 16

Anxious

Victoria

I sit out on the balcony watching the sun go down and close my eyes and take a deep breath. My stomach is in complete knots and it feels like I have been in the downward motion on a roller coaster for a little too long. My palms are starting to sweat as I try to practice my breathing technique. Breathe in – one-one thousand – breathe out – two-one thousand – this calms me a little bit but not enough for me to be ready for my date. I slowly repeat my breathing regimen, trying to keep from hyperventilating. What the hell did I just get myself into agreeing to go on a date with this extremely handsome man?

I shake out my fingers, trying to release the tension, and then run my fingers through my hair. I have got to pull it together or I won't make it through tonight. I know that this is what I wanted, but I am so nervous. I haven't been out with another man for the better part of ten years. I haven't had another man look at me and I look back, let alone touch me, or kiss me or make love to me. As that thought passes through my mind I am shocked. *Is that what I want?* For him to *kiss me, hold me, make love to me?* I feel myself start to moisten at the realization that something may happen between us tonight.

My skin quivers and starts to produce goosebumps at the thought of this glorious man touching my body. I massage the back of my neck using all of my strength. I have got to get this tension out of my muscles or I am going to be in physical pain. Almost as if she read my mind Tahj comes out to the balcony holding a bottle of Patron and two shot glasses. "How was your nap?" she inquired as she began to fill the shot glasses, thank the good Lord for liquid courage. I had been far too anxious to think of liquor as a solution. Tahj must have seen the look of panic on my face because she laughs and hands me a glass. "Bottoms up" we tap our glasses and take our shots.

"Got yourself in a little too deep didn't you" Tahj says with a smile… I am not sure how to react, so I respond the only way I know how, "I am hoping something goes deep tonight," I say with a wink. She sighs and rolls her eyes, "You are insufferable; I don't even know why I bother with you". We share a hearty laugh; it's amazing to me that she knows me so well. She pours me another… and another.

We have another conversation about my revelations this morning as we watch the sunset, the wind blowing our hair. She doesn't really say much as she takes in everything that I said. She pauses and then responds, "I would have liked for you to have done this differently; the right way". I look at her confused, is there a right way to do this? She laughs at me and explains further, "What I mean is if you had been legally separated from your husband. I

When Love Isn't Enough

would have liked for you to have figured out your situation before putting yourself into this position. You are my friend, my sister; and I love you. I support you no matter what you do. Just really think this through and make sure this is what you want." I nod as I take another shot, "I think whatever this is with Alex, is what I want. I am willing to bet everything that in this moment I am where I am supposed to be." She nods, seemingly satisfied as she hands me another shot. More upbeat then before she says, "Well if you like it I love it", we tap our glasses and down yet another shot.

    By this time my nerves have been replaced by anticipation. I haven't had to get ready for a proper date in a very long time. I almost forgot how much work went into getting ready. I jumped up almost knocking over the table which Tahj caught and steadied with her hand. "Whoa slow down tiger, where's the fire?" she says laughing. "I am going to be late. I only have an hour and a half before they get here.

When Love Isn't Enough

I run from the table to my room and start to fan through my clothes, which had been hung by the bellman in the closet; I don't have anything appropriate to wear. I start to panic again when there is a knock at the door. Tahj is standing there with two shopping bags; one garment bag and one a black shopping bag.

"I should not have napped earlier; I should have gone shopping with you. I don't have anything to wear! I am freaking out" I scream exasperated. Tahj laughs, "I figured you would say that. So, while I was shopping for myself I said 'self, I bet she did not bring clothes for a date because she was not expecting one'. While you were sleeping I was saving your life. This is my thank you for suggesting that we come on this trip." I stare at her in disbelief and she rolls her eyes and unzips the garment bag.

My eyes float to the dress that is exposed. It is absolutely beautiful! It is silk material and a beautiful cherry red color. It has a silk strap that wraps around the neck in a halter design. The top of the dress forms an A shape tightly hugging my chest, exposing the side of my body. The material wraps around into a deep cut that stops right above the small of my back. The bottom is mid-thigh length and hugs my hips just enough to be flattering. There is a piece of sheer, flowing material that comes almost to the floor in the back. My mouth drops and Tahj looks pleased with herself. "That's not all" she says as she hands me the black bag. I open it with my mouth still open and inside are: champagne colored heels that strap up in crisscross design, along with a matching handbag, "Tahj I can't take this. I have to pay you back".

She smiles a sincere smile, "This is a thank you. Thank you for always being there for me and making me come out of my comfort zone. Thank you for helping me see there is more to life. This is my gift to you"... I start to protest once more. This time she rolls her eyes and says, "You can and you will take it", puts the garment bags in my hand and walks out of the room. I giggle like a school girl as I hold the beautiful dress in my hands. I snatch the bag and run into the bathroom.

I jump in the shower and decide to linger there under the water for a few extra minutes as the water seers my skin, causing the muscles in my shoulders and back to relax. I bend the shower head to my will allowing it to massage the kinks out of my body. I turn it down a bit and decide to wash my hair (I want to go in my natural curls tonight).

After my shower is over I hold the dress once more, and stare at it. I put it on my body and it looks even more amazing on me than it does on the hanger (how is that even possible). It is the single most flattering dress I have ever worn, the silk material flows so perfectly over my curvaceous body, hugging me in all of the right places. Wow I think as I look at myself in the mirror, this is something that I wouldn't have worn before. I slide on the shoes. As I move they sparkle in the light. I have never seen anything like it.

I look at myself and I am inspired to do something different with my makeup. I dig deep into the bottom of my makeup bag to find something that not only compliments the dress, but also compliments how alive I feel. Deep in the corner of my makeup bag I find what I am looking for; a sparkling Amber eye shadow, a silver eyeshadow, gel eye liner, and red lipstick... *perfect*!

I start by placing the foundation on my face giving me a flawless complexion, and then I place the copper eye shadow on my eyes and fill my 'tear drop' with a shimmering white so that when I hit the light just right you catch a glimpse of it. I do a cat eye, with my liner and look at myself; my almond shaped eyes were the perfect shape for makeup. It was too bad that I didn't have time to do it back home. I don't even recognize myself! Last but not least I paint my lips red with lipstick; I look at myself and think of how stunning I look. It's not only the makeup that is hard to recognize, it is my eyes.

    The woman looking back at me looks happy, at peace. She looks alive for the first time in a very long time. I go into my jewelry bag and I grab some teardrop diamond earrings with a rose gold base that matches perfectly with my shoes. I slip back on my black diamond ring and smile thinking that I am going to need my girl Arya tonight. I think back to earlier today when I saw that black rose and it just let me know that she is here with me and for me. It was confirmation that she approved of where I am in my life and what I am about to do and that meant so much to me.

    I couldn't have picked out anything more perfect. I owe Tahj big time, I feel like an absolute princess. I switch my belongings into my new bag and I take one more look in the mirror. I can't believe how beautiful I look. I shake my head - shaking the image of the person that I was stepping foot on this island out of my mind. I did not want to be her any longer.

I go into the living room and I see Tahj coming out of her room. She has on a beautiful peacock blue silk dress that accentuates her physique perfectly. It looks as if the dress is made from two pieces of silk connected. One piece wraps once around her neck and covers the left part of her torso, sneaking softly over her arm. The other piece covers the right part of her torso and drapes exposing a slit from her neck to her navel. The bottom wraps around her body and as she walks it exposes her leg all the way up to her thigh. Her body is absolute perfection. She wears silver accessories that appear to be shimmering with diamonds and has spiked up her pixie cut with soft curls. She looks fantastic! How she is single is beyond me. We look at each other and share an embrace. We can't believe that we are about to do this... And then there is a knock at the door.

> "Thinking will not overcome fear. But action will."

> -W. Clement Stone

Chapter 17
Love At Second Sight

I open the door and Alex and Diego are standing on the opposite side. I try not to blush as I look at them because they are two of the most handsome men that I have ever laid eyes on. Diego looks as though he stepped straight out of a GQ magazine. He wore a pink fitted button up shirt that hugged every one of the muscles on his body, and fitted stone washed jeans that showed his large leg muscles. His look was finished off with a pair of brown faded designer boots and was accentuated by his clean shaven face; his slick black hair was spiked just a little.

The only thing that looked more appealing than Diego was Alex. Alex was considerably smaller in frame, but taller than Diego; and the way he carried himself made him seem larger than life. His eyes were enchanting and he wore a smile that was equally dazzling. I stared at his face for a little longer than what was socially acceptable, before assessing the rest of him (his face really was my favorite part). Finally, I noticed what he was wearing.

He wore a peacock blue button up shirt that was also fitted. It did not hug his frame as tightly as Diego's but I liked that about him; He left a lot to the imagination. He matched that with dark, distressed slender jeans that fit comfortably into his light grey loafers. He wore a shiny silver watch and he still donned the chain that showed the sun and the moon. This piqued my interest; *I will have to ask him about that later.* He was the model of perfection. His lips were the perfect shape and I wondered what they would feel like against mines; I exhaled.

I look up just in time to realize that he has been taking me in with his eyes; and he looks pleased with what he sees. We smile at each other and let out soft hellos.

When Love Isn't Enough

He smiles his brilliant smile and says "you are beautiful". I blush a little and respond "Igual". He takes my hand, "I have something special to show you". I look over at Tahj and see Diego kiss her hand and I see her let out a shy smile. We look at each other and grin; this was going to be an amazing night.

They take us down to the lobby and out the main doors where we are greeted first by the warm air and second by a chauffeur with the door extended. "After you mi Amor", I hear softly in my ear. I can't help but smile as I step inside the stretch limo. Everyone else followed suit and soon we were on our way. Even though I had no idea where we were going I feel completely safe.

We weave through the streets of Puerto Rico with the windows down and the occasional sound of music floods in from outside as we pass different bars. We talk the whole way there staring deeply into each other's eyes. I can't put my finger on it, but

I feel like I was starting to fall for him. I know it's impossible because it takes years to fall in love, right?

The limo finally came to a stop outside of a beautiful oceanfront restaurant with a sign out front that read Oceano's. He steps out first and grabs my hand helping me out. He wraps his hand around my waist and escorts me into the restaurant. He spoke to the hostess in Spanish and we are taken to our seats. Diego and Tahj sat a few tables over. When I asked why we did not all sit together? He said, it's because they wanted to spend time getting to know the real us. If we were together they would get the guarded versions of us.

We sit through a wonderful meal where we talked about: our families, my children, my relationship with my husband, his last relationship and then what we wanted out of life. It is magical! I look a few tables over to where Tahj and Diego are sitting. They look a little awkward, but they seem to be doing alright. I have not seen Tahj smile that much in a long time.

After dinner was over, he picks up the bill fold and pays – despite many protests from me. He responds "When you are out with me you don't pay"; I am not going to lie, it felt nice. We walk outside into the back of the restaurant where there was an outdoor bar and music playing. We have a few drinks out there and we got considerably more comfortable as the drinks kept flowing.

His hand finds my waist many times while we sit at the bar. We do not break eye contact as we continue to talk about everything that you could possibly imagine. Even though we do not speak the same native language we made it work. He spoke in English and when he couldn't think of the word he would tell me in Spanish, and I did the opposite. By the end of our conversation we had perfected "Spanglish" and I was suddenly grateful to my parents for making me take Spanish all those years.

When Love Isn't Enough

He leans into my ear and asks me if I like dancing. I tell him that I had two left feet (which was a lie, but I wanted him to be surprised when he saw me move). He says "no problem I will teach you". I smile, I liked the idea of him teaching me, and I would ease into the fact that I went to high school for dance and theatre. The limo pulls up and whisks us off into the night, our destination this time, a Salsa club called Club Brava.

We arrive at the club and I can barely contain my excitement. It was everything you saw in the movies but better. The men and women were dressed beautifully and the music was intoxicating. Tahj looks absolutely terrified, but I am in my element. He leads me immediately to the side of the crowded dance floor, eager to "teach" me. He starts out slowly, showing me the basic steps. I play along and let him think that he is showing me something new. After he is satisfied that he has taught me everything I need to know he leads me out to the middle of the dance floor.

When Love Isn't Enough

  I spin around him as the music played and he glows with delight. "You have been holding out on me Amor", we share a laugh as we danced around the floor. I look over at Tahj and she was taking it very slow over in the corner, she hates dancing. After a few more songs the DJ came on the mic and announces that he was going to play the Tango. He asked me if I knew how to dance to the Tango, I laugh, "Why don't you find out?" and grab his hand leading him back to the dance floor.

  This time the music is slow and seductive. We move slowly and provocatively at first; and then begin to whirl around the dance floor, dancing to the Argentine tango. My legs move faster than light and wrap around his body as we shared a quick kiss right there on the dance floor. We continue our seduction and I slowly slide down his body into a split on the floor. I see a hunger for my body looming in his eyes. He lifts me back into his arms and we kiss again. This time it's slow and rough just like the music playing in the background.

We whir around the floor with the red lights pulsating around us; our lips never parting. It wasn't until the song ended that we realized where we were.

    He grabs my hand and leads me off the dance floor. I dab my lips with a napkin to remove the excess moisture. He takes me to the bar and orders me a tequila sunrise. We stare at each other not saying anything, but feeling everything. Molecules in the air around us were moving so quickly that it felt like an electrical field was between our bodies! I was on fire. He leans into me and kisses me once more, softly biting my lips every other time our lips moved. I don't know what he is doing but I like it. He stops and smiles at me taking a sip of his drink and I followed suit taking a sip of mines.

    He came in for a kiss again but this time when our lips connect I feel a cool breeze coming from his mouth, followed by a piece of ice entering into mines. I was momentarily surprised but then I continue kissing him passing the ice back into his mouth. We continue like that for a few more minutes (replacing the ice once it had melted) unaware of our surroundings. Finally, he stops kissing me and says "I need to get you home. I want to see you again tomorrow for your last day here".

I nod slightly disappointed that the night has to come to an abrupt end. I ask him if he wants to stay and he says that he would if he could, but he has to work early tomorrow. He promises that we would be together tomorrow and kisses me on the forehead; signals to his brother and walks me outside holding my hand.

When we arrive at the hotel he kisses me goodbye and I watch the limo drive away. It was the first time Tahj and I have spoken all night, "What the hell was that?!?!?!?!" She says with a smirk on her face. I proceed to tell her about what happened that night and tell her we are planning to get together tomorrow night. She then fills me in on her night, reminding me that she hates dancing. She says she had a great time and they are also getting together tomorrow night. We end the night in our own beds - Alone. I wondered what would be happening if Alex had been here with me. With that thought I drift off to sleep and Alex haunts my dreams.

"Every moment spent with you is like a beautiful dream come true"

-Anonymous

Chapter 18

Paradise

```
Tahj
```

Victoria and I did not say much about what happened last night, but I knew it was because she was processing everything that had transpired. I knew that we would have the conversation when she was ready, so I was not going to push. We had just returned to the room from lunch and decided that we wanted to go to the pool bar before our dates tonight. We put on our swim suits and head out the door. As we walked along the beach I could hear the music coming from the bar.

When we arrive at the pool bar, we get into the water and walk over to the bar. The water is perfectly warm and the music contains the rhythmic beats of the island, adding to its allure. I strongly consider not going back home, then I sigh, thinking of my job and quickly abandon that idea. The bartenders are very attractive and vibrant. There are five of them fluttering back and forth behind the bar taking and filling orders. After getting the attention of one of the bartenders and ordering our drinks, Victoria and I share our thoughts about how nice it is here and then drift off into our own worlds as we sip our drinks.

My thoughts take me back to last night. Diego was so extremely handsome when I saw him at the door and I spent most of the night trying not to look at his body and how his shirt hugged him in all of the right places. Dinner started out a little awkward as we didn't really have much to talk about besides work. I am not an outgoing person so new conversations were hard for me. When we got to the bar things loosened up a little bit more as we talked through the basic small talk topics and realized we had a lot in common; Like our love for family and desire to have children.

When Love Isn't Enough

When we went to the salsa club I thought I was going to die because I had two left feet and I just knew it was going to go downhill from there; but I was pleasantly surprised. Victoria and Alex whirled all over the dance floor like they were on the season finale of dancing with the stars. Diego was content sitting there and watching with me, occasionally teaching me a move or two when his favorite songs came on.

I was pleased when he said that he wanted to see me again. After he gets off work we would go to dinner at the hotel and attend one of the shows there. I hated leaving Victoria here but I need to get dressed, my dinner reservation is in an hour. When I tell her goodbye and that I was going to get dressed she commented that it was only 4 o'clock. I told her that our show started at 6:30 so we had to have dinner at 5 o'clock. She gives me a hug and says that she would stay at the bar a little longer since she isn't going to dinner until 8 o'clock.

When Love Isn't Enough

When I got to the room I instantly got nervous. It hadn't occurred to me that I was going on a date alone with someone I actually like. That hasn't happened in a really long time. I turn on the water and get underneath, allowing it to run over my body. I hear my alarm going off telling me it was time to get dressed. I hurry through the rest of my shower, brush my teeth and do my hair. I slip into the black dress I had laid out on the bed and put on a pair of strappy black heels.

No sooner than I finish putting on my makeup there is a knock on the door. I grab my purse and rush to the living area. I am going to have to relax if I wanted to make it through tonight. I take a deep breath and open the door; on the other side of the door stands Diego, looking just as handsome as the day before.

He has on a black T-Shirt that hugs his muscles, dark jeans and black dress shoes. He leans in to give me a kiss on the cheek and I catch a whiff of his cologne, which caused me to inhale very deeply. *Damn he smells good.* He pulls a bouquet of colorful flowers from behind his back and hands them to me. I smile at this gesture, it is the sweetest thing that any guy had done for me in a very long time. I excuse myself to put the flowers into some water and when I return he holds my hand as we walk to the restaurant.

Tonight went a lot more smoothly than yesterday. The conversation between us flowed well through dinner and we share a lot of laughs. He tells me about his dreams of being a chef and I tell him a little bit more about work – but not too much because I do not want to scare him off. After dinner we attend a show at the hotel that featured a musical performance and dancers. We dance and sing, quite badly - I might add - to a lot of songs that were very popular in the States.

After the show we walk out to the beach and find some seats, where we sit and talk for hours about everything! He is so

When Love Isn't Enough

patient and caring and wants to know so much about me. I have not had that kind of quality conversation in a very long time. Most of the guys that I met and dealt with back home were so self-centered, that even when they asked you about your day it was just used as a platform to somehow interrupt you and tell you about theirs. The most wonderful, and at the same time, insulting thing about my time with him, is that he has not tried to kiss me yet. Wonderful because it showed a certain level of respect towards me, insulting because it felt like maybe he wasn't attracted enough to me to try.

I sigh, and in his truly attentive nature he caught it and asks me what's wrong, I lie and told him "nothing". "You are not enjoying yourself with me tonight?" He asks. "I am having a wonderful time; I am just thinking that I am sad I have to leave tomorrow. I am going to miss Puerto Rico" ... I pause, hesitating while I deliberate whether or not to allow myself to be vulnerable, by continuing my thought.

When Love Isn't Enough

"Dime", he says breaking the silence, "What does that mean?" I reply confused. "It means tell me", I look into his eyes and see the level of sincerity in them and decide to continue with the truth. "I am going to miss spending time with you" I say as I looked down towards the ground. His reply sent quivers through my body "Yeah, I am pretty sad that you are leaving, but that just means that we will just have to work harder to see each other". I look up, shocked "You want to see me again?" "Of course!" he replies, "I have truly enjoyed getting to know you. I have not met anyone like you and I want to get to know you better... if you will let me". I smile as I stare into his eyes, "I would like that" and I lean in to kiss him gently under the moonlight.

When Love Isn't Enough

"Those who live passionately teach us how to love. Those who love passionately teach us how to live"

-Sarah Ban Breathnach

Chapter 19

This Is What It Feels Like

Victoria

I drank a little too much at the bar to calm my nerves about tonight. I waited until the last minute and made my way back to the room. I took a hot shower to work the tension out of my shoulders and I decided to shave everything, just in case. After I finished my shower I dried off and put lotion all over my body and sprayed on my favorite perfume, Forever Red, from Bath and Body Works.

I take deep breaths as I brush my teeth and apply my makeup. I slip on a pink flowy dress and flat sandals and massage my neck once more, to relieve some last minute tension and grab my purse. I go to the kitchen to take a shot of tequila when there is a knock at the door. I take a deep breath and open the door. There he stood, just as handsome as the first time I met him. He wore a light blue shirt, and light skinny jeans, with grey loafers. He also had that necklace on his neck again.

I can't take my eyes off of him. My assessment of him is interrupted by his husky, deeply accented, "Hello Amor". I look up and he leans in to kiss me. His lips were so soft and I am instantly reminded of last night and it sent chills through my body. He has a bag in his hand that he wants to place in the room. He says that he will come back and pick it up later. I find this strange, but tell him that he can leave it in my bedroom.

He places the bag in my room and leads me to dinner with a hand wrapped around my waist. We are having another wonderful conversation when he tells me that he has strong feelings towards me and does not want me to leave tomorrow. "I can't stay, I wish I could but I have responsibilities back home" I reply, surprising myself by the sadness in my voice. He responds "I understand. Well we always have tonight and we will see what follows after that".

After dinner, we hold hands and walk across the resort back to my room. He tells me he has a surprise for me but he needs me to leave him in the bedroom so that he can "set it up". I hesitantly agree and lead him into the bedroom giving him a kiss before I walk out. I sit on the couch in the living area for a while but I get anxious; so I make my way into Tahj's bathroom and freshen up and touch up my makeup. I make my way to the balcony and open the door.

The air was warm on my skin and because it was nighttime, the water came further up the shoreline. Every time a large wave crashes I can feel a small amount of salt water hit my face. I look out over the water illuminated by the moon and stars that paint the sky. I close my eyes and take in all of these memories saddened by the thought that I would be home tomorrow.

When Love Isn't Enough

I feel his presence behind me before he touches me. He places his hand on the small of my back with the tiniest amount of pressure. I turn around to see him holding a glass of wine in his hand for me. I take it from him skeptically; he looks perplexed by my response. "I want to switch glasses with you, just to make sure that you aren't trying to drug me" I say sternly. He laughs hysterically but obliges me "Look Amor, I will even take a sip first". I laugh and take a sip of my drink. It is exquisite! The robust body of the wine fills my taste buds and alerts my senses. We sit in silence drinking our wine and looking out over the water.

After I finish my glass of wine he takes it from me and sets it on the table, telling me to come with him. When I walk in the door there are rose petals that lead to the bedroom. Small tea light candles line the pathway of roses. I stand there shocked with my mouth open. "How... How did you pull this off? You did all of this for me?" I say with tears in my eyes. He wipes the tears from my eyes and replies, "That bag that I brought in earlier. It had everything that I needed to make this a special night for you; because you are a special woman and you deserve it."

"When I told you I had feelings for you... I meant it. I think I am falling in love with you, even though I know it is not possible to feel all of these emotions so soon. I know we cannot be together, but my heart does not want to listen to that, Now, follow me Princess". He leads me into the bedroom which is dark with the exception of candles he had carefully placed all over the room. There is soft music playing in the background and more roses on the bed.

A small tear formed in the corner of my eye. No one has ever done anything this nice for me before. He takes my hand and leads me to the bathroom where there is a negligée hanging on the back of the door. "I bought it for you and I think it's your size. Please put it on and come out when you are ready" he says backing out of the bathroom and closing the door.

When Love Isn't Enough

I breathe deeply in anticipation of what is about to happen to me. I hurriedly put on the lingerie before I lose my nerve and look at myself in the mirror in the lacy black dress. I notice how beautiful I look as I fluff my hair. I take a deep breath and open the door. I look around the room and notice he is near the bed and there was a blindfold placed in the middle. He grabs the blindfold, walks over to me, and places it over my eyes.

At the loss of my eyesight the rest of my senses kick into overdrive. He sat me on the bed prompting me to lie down on my stomach. I breathe deeply at the touch of his hand on my body. He places warm oil on my body and begins massaging it into the skin on my back. He continues this ritual until he has rubbed oil on every inch of my exposed skin.

He flips me over onto my back and kisses me softly from my head to my breasts. He spends a little time there slowly massaging one of my breasts with his hand

and the other he massages with his tongue. He moves up my chest placing small kisses all the way to my mouth.

He kisses me deeply and roughly which launches my body into action. I thought that because I couldn't see him it would somehow take away from the experience; but it only intensified it. He left my lips and starts to make a trail down the middle of my body with his tongue, stopping only when he got between my legs. He takes my hand and places it at my opening to separate my lips and hold them in place, so that he had a clear access.

He licks me, slowly at first and then increases his intensity. He moves his tongue in ways that I did not even know possible: vibrating, twirling, fast, and slow. He grabs my clit lightly between his teeth ... I grip the covers and curl my toes, moaning loudly. He did not stop until I could not take it anymore and exploded with pleasure.

When he was satisfied with the work he had done, I felt him get out of the bed. I

When Love Isn't Enough

sit there panting heavily as I feel the weight of him return to the bed, causing the bed to shift. He took off the blindfold while kissing me. He must have gotten up to wipe his face because it was dry, and I was appreciative. He kisses me deeply and gets up to put on a condom. He looks at me and says, "Do I have your permission to enter you?" I nod in too much pleasure to speak. I grab his head and pull his mouth back to mine. With that confirmation, he enters me.

"Sometimes giving someone a second chance is like giving them an extra bullet for their gun because they missed you the first time."

-Heartfeltquotes.blogspot.com

Chapter 20

Making Up Is Never Easy

Desi

I woke up this morning with my bruises starting to yellow. It's been about a week since the latest episode with my husband and he hasn't been sleeping at my house. He has no doubt been off with his little bitch. But I know I have to get up and get moving for my children. I made up some lame excuse as to why they needed to go stay with grandma. The worst part about all of this is that I am suffering in silence. It's not like I don't have people in my life that would care if I told them. It's just that I am too proud to admit I made a mistake.

I am ashamed, because I allowed my life to become this, because I enjoy my lifestyle. I am ashamed that I put myself on the back burner because I like nice shit. I don't even know where to start; I just can't

When Love Isn't Enough

tell them yet. It's not time and I am just not ready. I am not mentally ready for what my life is going to be like when this happens.

As I go into the bathroom, I catch a glimpse of myself in the mirror as I pass by. I don't even recognize this girl. I don't recognize her with this black eye, bruised lip, scars all over my body... marks that cannot be love. But, I already have plans to meet with the girls; I've brushed them off a couple of times already. If I don't go they will come see me and I am just not ready. I put on some of the most expensive makeup that I could find, that provided full coverage. With every stroke of my foundation brush I covered the pain. I covered the memories. I covered the sorrow. I covered the disappointment. I covered the truth.

As I painted this mask on my face, this mask of happiness; I hide behind this veil that is my perfect life. I slide on my dress, one arm, over the other and it's very sore. As I pull the strap up over my arm, I

When Love Isn't Enough

touch all of the bruises and all of the spots that my husband, my love, *humph*, left on my body. I realized that I have missed a spot and I fall to the ground. Sad. Broken. I can't do this; I can't go on pretending to be happy. How do I do this... again? How do I pick up these broken pieces... again?

Something catches my eye in the mirror. I look up and it's my husband. He has something in his hand and I don't know what it is. I am scared. He comes over to me and hands me a box, reaches his hand out to me to help me up. As he helps me up he takes his finger so gently and wipes the tears from under my eyes. How can this be the same man? His hands so gentle; so comforting. I cup my face into his palm as I wept. How can this be the same person? I don't understand how this is the same man.

He tells me, "Honey open the box", I let out a sigh as my body shivers, I breathe heavily and I open the box in my hand, after running my fingers along the outside. Inside is the most beautiful canary diamond bracelet and necklace that I have ever seen. I begin to weep and I tell him that I can't take it.

"I am so sorry; I don't know what came over me. I have so much stress at the office. My mother is sick. I have been fighting with my brother. I need you and I am so sorry. I will get help, I will go to counseling. I will do whatever you need me to do, just don't leave me. We saw these when we were in St. Thomas at a jewelry store. I knew you liked them so I flew all the way to St. Thomas to get them for you. That's where I have been. Please do me the honor of wearing them. I know you will look lovely and they will match perfectly with the gold and black dress that you are wearing."

He gently brushes the hair off of my shoulders; so softly that it could have almost been a feather. He puts that canary diamond on my neck and as he goes to put the bracelet on my wrist he comes across the bruises from where he grabbed my wrist.

When Love Isn't Enough

He kisses it, picks up the foundation and concealer that I have been placing all over my body and he takes it and brushes it over my bruises. You can't see them anymore.

"I will never hurt you again", he says as he places the delicate bracelet on my wrist. "When you are done with your friends, I want to pamper you. I want to cater to you when you come home. I am so sorry and thank you for standing by me". I feel like such a fool for believing him. God I wanted to believe him. I wanted to believe that this time is different. This time he meant it. This time... this time he will get the help. He will change and be the man that he was in the beginning of our relationship.

I grab my purse and he kisses me on the forehead and I catch myself staring at my new diamonds. For a moment I think what a lucky girl I am and in the same breath my voice, my inner voice, is telling me *you're a fool if you believe him!* I am just not ready yet. I know he loves me and I just need more time.   With one final glance in the mirror I walk out the door.

"The Best Mirror is an old friend"

-George Herbert

Chapter 21

Sydney's Wine Bar

Arya

Today the girls are meeting at Sydney's wine bar. It is a very modern bar in the heart of Uptown Charlotte. Most nights there is live music playing but tonight will be quieter; which they wanted since they had not had a chance to catch up. So much has happened since the last time they were all together. I go over to the table and today Victoria was the first to arrive - which is completely abnormal and has everyone but Tahj wondering what is going on.

Everyone sips their wine waiting for someone else to talk. Alayna went first, "I slept with Antonio". There were gasps across the table, "Like your friend Antonio?" asks Desi. "Yes, one and the same" says Alayna. "Well what the hell happened there? I thought he had a girlfriend", says

When Love Isn't Enough

Tahj. Alayna proceeds to tell them what happened between him and his girlfriend, and what happened when he came to her house. She also tells them about the conversation that happened the next day. "So what's been happening since the conversation?" asks Victoria. "Well we have actually been dating. He has taken me to dinner a few times and to the movies. We have gone bowling and just hung out at his house and mines. It actually feels like we are a real couple".

All of the girls seem pleased by this information. Alayna looks and appears to be pondering something... after a few moments all of the other girls catch on. "What is it Alayna. Everything sounds like it is going well?" asks Desi. Alayna takes a deep breath and answers her, "I am glad that everything is going well... it's just that. Well it's just that I think... I think I might be pregnant, my period is late". Everyone shares shocked glances across the table but Desi is the first to speak, "Really Alayna, how could you be so stupid! That man was practically married to his girlfriend and you just go and get pregnant by him? How do you know he is not just using you until she comes back? How do you know that this is even something real? Why couldn't you have waited until you were married or hell at least in a relationship with him?" Victoria and Tahj shot Desi disapproving glances, to which she responded by rolling her eyes.

Tahj said to Alayna in a very calm voice, "Well I support you no matter what and as long as you are happy we are happy for you." Victoria cosigned with a nod, "Desi just needs to realize that everyone can't have things laid out perfectly like she does and doesn't have the perfect life. Desi looked away with her nose turned up and changed the subject, "So how was the trip?"

Tahj glanced at Victoria, who gave her a warning glance, but Tahj continued telling her story of how she met Diego and the dates they went on and their plans to see each other again. The girls asked her a few more questions, which she answered with a smile. Alayna said with a smile, "You really like this guy don't you? I can't remember the last time I saw you like this". Tahj blushed, "I really do. I don't know what it is about him but he is special".

Alayna probed Victoria, "Don't think we didn't catch that look you gave Tahj! What the hell was that about? What happened when you were on your trip?" Victoria sighed, she had been busted. She took a deep breath and then told them about what had been happening with her husband. She told them about Alex and the dates that they went on, the dancing, and the kisses they shared. She paused and when there wasn't immediate outrage, she continued. She told them about the romantic evening they had on her last night on the island and them making love.

Alayna sat there with her mouth wide open and a sheepish grin, and Tahj just sipped her wine (having already been filled in on the details on their plane ride back). Desi responded, "Are you fucking kidding me? You are just going to cheat on Max like that? Do you know how hard it is to find a good man out here and you have one and are just going to throw it all away for some fuck fest on the beach? Some booty call that is never going to call you back! You should be completely ashamed of yourself for whoring around on that island. You are somebody's wife and mother and you should act accordingly! If you are going to shit on your husband you might as well give him up to some woman that will appreciate him more than you. You don't deserve him!" she pushed her chair away from the table and stormed out.

Victoria sat there with tears in her eyes and her mouth open; for the first time she was speechless. Alayna looked horrified at Desi's response and grabbed Victoria's hand, "Listen Victoria, I don't agree with what you did, but I can completely understand doing something that makes you feel alive for the first time in a long time. I don't know what it's like to be married; but I do know what it's like to feel invisible and unwanted. That is not a feeling I would wish on my worst enemy.

I am sorry that you have had to live with that feeling for so long. You know I love you and only want you to be happy. I will say that I haven't seen you as happy as you were while you were telling your story, in a very long time. I think you made the right decision for yourself as a woman. I am going to go see what the hell is going on with Desi because her response was completely inappropriate. She has a huge stick up her ass about something" Alayna got up from the table and went to find Desi.

Tahj just reached over and hugged Victoria who sobbed into her shoulder. "The sad thing is that I don't even regret it. I would do it again if I had the chance. What does that mean?" Tahj thought carefully and replied to Victoria, "It means that you have a lot to think about and I think you have to tell Max what happened." "You are right" Victoria replied, paused and then continued "I am so pissed at Desi, I may not have made

When Love Isn't Enough

the choice that she would have made but she had no right to crucify me like that. I would never judge her that way. Everyone can't have a perfect life like her, with the perfect husband", she says with malice in her voice. Victoria dries her eyes and looks out the window, thinking about what she is going to do next.

"Walking with a friend in the dark is better than walking alone in the light"
-Helen Keller

Chapter 22

What's Words Between Friends?

Alayna

I found Desi sitting outside on a bench smoking a cigarette. I didn't even know that she smoked. I have never seen Desi become this unhinged before. I mean she has always been slightly judgmental but never to the point where she was calling us names and being disrespectful. Even though she completely offended me, I know that something is wrong and as her friend I owe it to her to find out what's going on.

I walk over to the bench and sit down next to her. We just stare at the passing traffic for a few minutes in silence. When she finishes her cigarette she lit up another one and sighs, "This is a horrible habit that I picked up about six months ago… Right around the time I first found out that my husband was cheating on me." I turn to stare at her with a look of complete shock on my face, but still I say nothing. I had no idea, Desi always put on this image that her life was perfect.

She continues, "I knew he was cheating about six months ago but I didn't want to confront my husband because I thought maybe it was a phase and he would end it on his own. Three weeks ago I found lipstick on his collar and could no longer ignore it because he was getting sloppy". She laughs an almost defeated laugh. "Do you know what happened when I confronted him about it?" There was long pause, but I didn't dare interrupt for fear of her losing her nerve.

"He beat the shit out of me", she sighed. I let out a gasp "Desi! Are you fucking kidding me?" She starts to cry, "No I am not kidding you. It has been going on for a few years now but I didn't want to say anything, because I didn't want people to judge me. I feel like I had to tell you today because I need you to understand that my anger is not at you and Victoria. I behaved poorly because I am angry with myself for allowing it to get this bad. To be perfectly honest, I am actually jealous of Victoria for having the guts to do something like that for her own sanity. I am so sorry Alayna for saying those things to you; I didn't mean any of it".

"Desi, you are already forgiven. I am so sorry that you have had to go through all of this by yourself. You should have told us sooner. We would have supported you and been there for you. Does anyone else know?" Alayna asked. "No", Desi sobbed, "You are the first person that I have told". I looked down at the ground with the weight of what Desi has just told me heavy on my heart. On the ground near the bench I notice a black rose.

"Arya" I say out loud. Desi looks up shocked and then follows my gaze. She lets out a small laugh between sobs, "I should have known she was here and that is why I am blabbing all of my business". At this realization we both laugh. "I miss her so much", I exclaim, "She was my best friend when I had no one", "Mines too" says Desi. We look at each other and share a much needed hug.

"You have to tell the others", I tell Desi. "Victoria will probably never speak to me again for me to apologize, and I don't blame her" Desi sighs. "She will; she just needs to understand what is going on with you. She loves you and I know she will forgive you. She would never want you to go through this alone. We are your sisters; we will get through all of this together". With a glance down at the black rose, Desi reaches down to pick it up and looks at me with a determination in her eyes, "Okay."

We make our way back into the bar and I have my arm around her and she shakes badly with nerves. We walk back to the table and I see Victoria shift uncomfortably. Tahj gets ready to light into Desi until she sees the rose in her hand and that stops her dead in her tracks. Tahj just stares at the Black Rose in Desi's hand and says nothing.

Victoria, refusing to look in Desi's general area, does not realize what is happening. Desi breaks the silence, "I saw a piece of Arya today". Victoria looks up at the mention of Arya's name and notices the rose in Desi's hand. Her look softens from hurt and disappointment to love. Desi hands her the rose and continues. She told Victoria and Tahj about what has been happening with her husband and says that she cannot live in silence and fear any longer. Both Tahj and Victoria have expressions of sadness followed by anger.

After they ask Desi all the same questions I asked her, they were ready to get up from the table and go whoop his ass. Desi stops them, "I need to do this on my own. I wanted to tell you because I don't want to be emotionally isolated any longer. I need my sisters to help me get through this darkness. You have to let me find my way out of this situation on my own. I promise I

When Love Isn't Enough

will tell you if I need something more than your love and support, but right now that is all I need. Promise me you will let me figure this out. Promise me you will love me through it. I promise you that I will let you know when I am in over my head".

    Desi shoots a pleading glance around the table. Victoria and Tahj share an angry glance, but ultimately agree. "If we get the first sense that something is wrong, and you disappear or are not answering our calls... we are going after him!" Victoria adds and Tahj nods in agreement. Desi walks over to Victoria, "I am so sorry for..." but she is shushed by Victoria who is already out of her seat hugging her. "Thank you for speaking your mind; I love you for that... Just don't do it again!" We all shared a laugh. The mood lightened and we sat huddled together on the same side of the table, sharing stories and talking for hours. The sun succumbed to the darkness when we went our separate ways home.

We were left with a lot of information and thoughts of the future. We were left wondering what was going to happen with Tahj and her mystery man. What was going to happen between Victoria and Max, Victoria and Alex? What was going to happen with Desi and Daniel? As for me, I will be going home to take a pregnancy test…

It's amazing what happens every time I get together with my friends… my sisters.

When Love Isn't Enough

"There are wounds that never show on the body that are deeper and more hurtful than anything that bleeds"

-Laurell K. Hamilton

Chapter 23

What's Done In The Dark

Desi

As my husband slept his phone started to buzz. That intrigued me; normally he leaves his ringer on. Why was it on vibrate? Was it just because he got back from working out? Or he was tired? After his last little episode he assured me that he had stopped talking to her and that he loved only me. He told me he had moved on and wasn't doing anything wrong anymore. He swore to me that he was done. So why was his phone on vibrate?

There is literally no reason to put your phone on vibrate on a Saturday, when you are not at work. All of my Spidey senses started going off. I knew that something was not right. I quietly walk over to his phone; afraid that if I woke him the consequences would be grave for me. I look

When Love Isn't Enough

at the notification screen – see men are not that smart, if you are going to be doing dirt remove your notifications so people can't see it pop up on the screen. Never the less several messages popped up on his notification screen, some of which contained pictures, from somebody named Felicia.

    I knew I shouldn't dig and the last time we had a conversation about this ended very badly for me. I need to know why this bitch was sending my husband pictures in the middle of the afternoon. Curiosity got the best of me and I decided it was worth the risk and consequences to find out the truth. My husband had an IPhone so I was hoping and praying he had been stupid enough to set his fingerprint recognition for his passcode. I take his phone and slid it gently under his hand as he slept and placed his thumb on the home button. If my husband woke up while I was doing this he was going to kill me. The dots filled the screen and the phone screen opened up to reveal his apps. *Yes*!!!

It worked! I went to his text message app and clicked on Felicia's name and all of their messages popped up. The first thing that I noticed caused my heart to drop to the floor... NO!NO!NO!!! Why is she sending this to him! Please God let this be a mistake or let her just be a friend that he is not sleeping with... but I don't have to wonder long.

My worst fears are confirmed by her very next text message. "I just thought you should know", was the caption that followed the ultra sound pictures in the previous texts. I sank into the chair in the corner just trying to take everything in while simultaneously coaching myself through breathing. *Deep breath in, deep breath out.* Repeat. What the hell is happening here?

I need more information to fully process what I am reading as the blood starts to rush through my head... I continue to read. Three weeks ago a message that reads. "I had a great time in St. Thomas this weekend. You have to take me back sometime". A few days later another message "You haven't come home yet! Where are you? You had better not be with her". The next day "You told me you were leaving her and that is why you had me put up in this condo, so we could be together. How could you go back to her after I left my boyfriend to be with you?" Then three days ago "I knew you couldn't' stay away! I loved having you inside of me again! I missed you". Then a response from him... "I missed being with you. You make me feel so different, so special, I have never felt like this about any other woman, don't contact me for a while... Just give me some time to get out of this situation and we will be together soon. I love you." Then nothing until this... "I just thought you should know". Those words burned like a branding iron to my heart.

    I should have known he wasn't going to change. I should have known he would do the same shit over and over again. Why did I ever believe he could change? That he actually wanted to change? How could I be so stupid? The truth of my fucked up reality is that I have spent the last three years of my relationship being abused. The first year was only mental and emotional abuse. He would say things to make me feel insignificant and undesirable. He isolated me from everyone I cared about – except for my girlfriends because they would not allow it. At first his words rolled off my back and I didn't believe them. Then they started to hold a little more weight in my psyche until I felt that I would be nothing without him and I should consider myself lucky.

Then it got physical, first it started with a push; then him grabbing me; then a slap; then a punch; then a beating. Every time he was sorrier than the last and went to greater lengths to get me to forgive him. He would behave longer in between. Recently, I have been getting severe beatings every other week. I kept forgiving him because at first I believed it was me that caused these reactions; I was somehow being a bad wife, and I wasn't being a good Catholic woman by complaining about my husband.

When Love Isn't Enough

    I couldn't talk to my family because as a Hispanic woman the objective was to marry a man that was the head of the household and was the bread winner. My husband did everything for my family, so I would be disowned for speaking against him. Not to mention talking about domestic violence was very taboo in my house growing up.

    I couldn't talk to my friends because I knew they would never let this continue and I did not want their looks of pity. Similar to the looks they gave me a few weeks ago when I opened up to them for the first time, about the issues with my husband. Right after I exploded on Victoria and stormed out.

    I have put up with a lot of shit from this man, but this was unforgivable. This ultrasound was of a pretty developed baby, this was not a new pregnancy. I looked at the ultrasound and could distinguish a pretty good amount of body parts. . I looked for the pregnancy date information on the ultrasound picture, but it had been cropped out. However, it didn't take an OBGYN to know that this baby was at least in the second trimester. *I mean, he should have known if she was pregnant by now right? Maybe this is some sort of mistake.*

    I held onto the tiniest bit of hope; but that hope was quickly dashed. Almost as soon as I had that thought another message came through, "I know you told me not to contact you but I thought you would want to know about our baby". *Oh hell no!* This man went and got this chick pregnant. *Naw Fuck that*, I am done! Now my original response was to wake his ass up and light him on fire! Then my better judgment kicked in. That would probably result in me getting beat and him somehow spinning it before deleting the evidence so that I could not access it any longer.

    He went through great lengths to keep me from finding any solid proof of him cheating because of our prenuptial agreement. Our pre-nup states that if the cause of the dissolution of our marriage was infidelity on his part, then I am guaranteed half of his assets. If the marriage is dissolved for any other reason, I get nothing except for a pre-determined amount of child support. Now that I think back on that, I should never have signed that pre-nup; but I was young, dumb and in love with someone I was never planning on leaving. I knew I needed to keep my cool about this until I could secure the evidence and ensure my safety; I decided to play this smart.

    I forwarded those text messages to myself, as well as the screenshots that I took of photos on his phone screen (so he could not deny later that it came from his phone). I marked those messages as unread so that he would have no idea they had been read. I then deleted the sent messages. It's time to go see my lawyer. It's time to get all of this on record so this bastard can't deny it. He can't hurt me trying to stop me from presenting this evidence against him. I might be nice and not kill his reputation in the process.

When Love Isn't Enough

That's the thing about powerful men like Daniel; they have an Achilles heel ... and that is their reputation. He cares so much about what other people think about him that he would never want me to taint his image with a scandal. He would rather kill me first. This was my way out. Thank you Felicia!

I recorded all of her contact information, logged into Verizon from his phone, and downloaded a copy of his phone records and sent it to myself as well. I am going to do some research and take all of this information to the lawyer. With this infidelity and the evidence I have collected against him; his pre-nup no longer stands.

With a lawyer having all of this information protected, he will know that if anything happens to me this information will be leaked to the public. He will be charged in whatever crime was committed against me. I had never really wanted to bury Daniel before because I loved him and wanted to make this marriage work. This situation has caused me to re-evaluate my standing in this marriage. This time, I am not emotional. This time I am thinking clearly. I got his ass!

TO BE CONTINUED...

Epilogue
The Rebirth

When Love Isn't Enough

Arya Rose

As I wander down the street once more, I reflect on all of the things that we have been through as friends... While I was here on this earth, and after; I reflect on all of the changes that have happened and come to a realization. Before, I thought the black of the rose symbolized: emptiness, loneliness, darkness, pain, sadness, fear and death. I have learned that the black of the rose symbolizes rebirth! It symbolizes a new life, happiness and resurrection from the ashes. I have learned that black symbolizes strength because it can consume everything else around it. So now, when I see the black rose on the side of the road, I am no longer afraid that it is ominous, I am hopeful. It means something new to me! It means new life; it means a new future and it means a rebirth.

When Love Isn't Enough

About The Author

Ella has always wanted to be in a position to help people. As an undergraduate student at the University of Minnesota – Twin Cities she studied Sociology of Law-Criminology and Deviance. Her objective was to become a lawyer but as she began the application process she realized that her heart wasn't in it and continued to pursue her professional career. She has worked in Human Resources, Retail and Banking in management capacities and continued to help people in various ways. She received her Master's Degree from the University of Wisconsin – Milwaukee in Human Resources hoping to further her desire to help people. There was always a burning desire to do more and none of the paths ever seemed to be quite right.

One day as she was talking to one of her girlfriends having an issue and she contemplated her own life and realized there was a way she could help people (women in particular). She could help them by providing them a voice and addressing issues that real women face every day. She wanted them to know that it's ok to have feelings and struggle sometimes, that they are not alone. It can be difficult to bring these issues to the forefront. That's when Tahj, Victoria, Alayna, Desi and Arya Rose were born. She wrote their story by placing herself in their shoes (she was previously an actress) and telling their story in the way only a group of girlfriends can. As a diverse group of friends they are able to address a lot of issues within the realm of safety brought by girlfriends. Through this platform Ella was able to live her dream of helping people on a much larger scale by writing to their souls. She currently resides in Charlotte, NC with her husband and their daughter.

When Love Isn't Enough

Contact the Author

www.Ella-York.com

Email:

Rashida@ella-york.com

Twitter:
www.Twitter.com/TheEllaYork

Facebook:
www.Facebook.com/TheEllaYork

When Love Isn't Enough

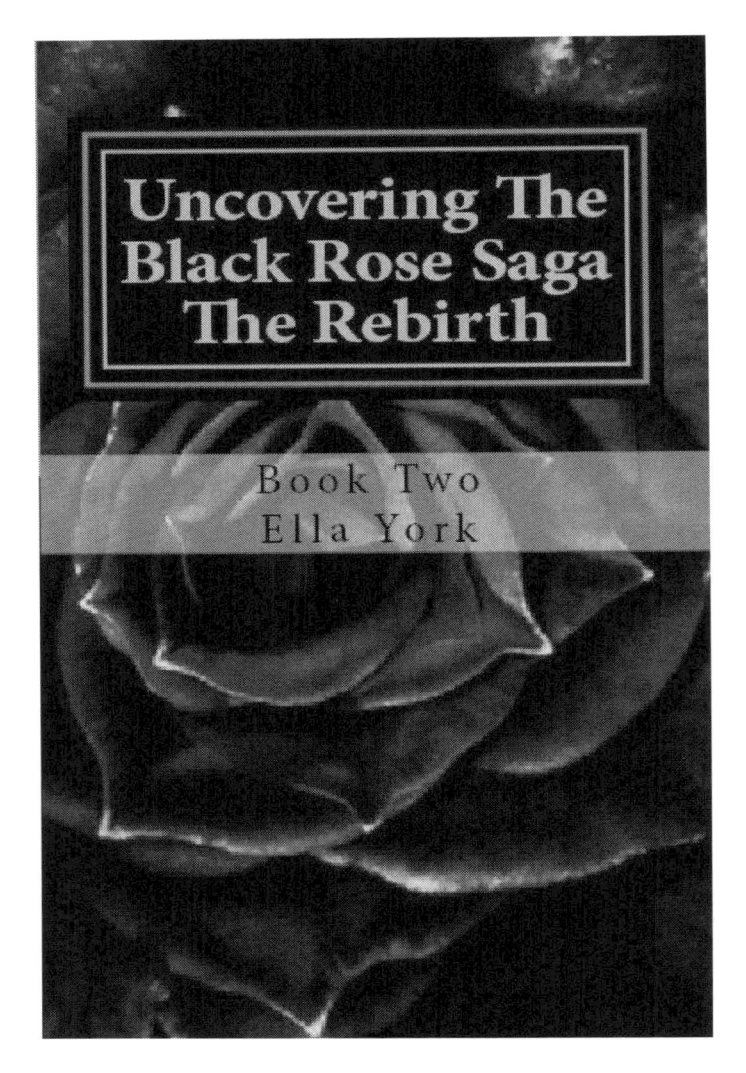

Uncovering The Black Rose Saga
The Rebirth

Book Two
Ella York

Coming Soon